THE
ACQUISITION

THE
ACQUISITION

AURA POLANCO

THE ACQUISITION

iUniverse books may be ordered through booksellers or by contacting:

iUniverse
1663 Liberty Drive
Bloomington, IN 47403
www.iuniverse.com
1-800-Authors (1-800-288-4677)

ISBN: 978-1-5320-0447-6 (sc)
ISBN: 978-1-5320-0448-3 (e)

Library of Congress Control Number: 2016913198

Print information available on the last page.

iUniverse rev. date: 08/27/2016

To my parents

Acknowledgements

Some years ago, my dear friend and mentor, Susan Lessor-Guzman encouraged me to pursue my interest in writing. She knew of my potential having been a former teacher of mine. I mulled the idea over and after perusing through several dusty writing pieces I had tucked away in a box over the years, I took this leap of faith. I thank her for igniting a fire that had burnt out long ago and that is now ablaze. Also, I cannot thank my love, Rafael, enough for his encouragement, ideas and inspiration. I love the text work you did for the cover. You are that light that so brightly burns in me now. To all the incredible editors, production and support staff at iUniverse. You were at my beck and call and always so professional and helpful. My parents have had an unwavering love and support for me since I was a child. I thank them for allowing me to scribble for hours on end and encourage my imagination to flourish. And to my little Lola, just simply, thank you.

Contents

PART ONE

CHAPTER 1

Humiliated

Valentina waited off to the side carrying the heavy crystal and chrome award. She traced her finger over his name without much thought as she waited for Marcus to return with her wrap from the coat check. Seven other employees of Infinity Acquisitions including board members had gathered at the Waldorf Astoria Ballroom to celebrate Marcus receiving the Prestigious Arts and Preservations Council Award for his work in preserving New York City landmarks.

The warm evening gave way to groups of people huddling outside the famous landmark hotel to await their cars. Amongst these groups was the small team from Infinity congratulating Marcus and chatting about banal matters. Feeling tired and quite buzzed after downing one too many cocktails Valentina bid everyone a good night and quietly moved away to hail a cab when Marcus came up to her.

"I'll drop you off at your place."

"Oh, you sure because I figured you wanted to continue partying with the board members."

"Are you serious? I would rather know you are home safe. Besides I have a breakfast meeting with Woolsley. Come with me, please."

1

It was not uncommon for Valentina and Marcus to be at the same social gatherings representing their company, as he was her boss and she a respected Estates and Acquisitions purveyor. They also often shared rides back to their respective homes because they lived within a ten-block radius.

Valentina took this opportunity because she was having a difficult time navigating on five-inch heels and she could use the strength and comfort that Marcus exuded. She took his hand and carefully stepped into the car to avoid ripping her long gown or tripping on the ridiculously high heels. Within minutes she was asleep from the rolling of the car. To keep her head from dangerously lolling back and forth Marcus moved closer to her and gently rested it on his shoulder. For Marcus, this closeness was a moment he cherished. As the car sped up Third Avenue, Marcus thought back to what Diana Monroe whispered in his ear at the awards ceremony about the announcement coming out in tomorrows New York Times. He knew how much this news would devastate Valentina yet could not think of a way to buffer the inevitable blow that awaited his secret love.

Moving her gently he called, "Valentina, Valentina, we're here. Wake up." He shook her gently as she opened her eyes and realized where she was.

"Oh my God. I'm so embarrassed. Sorry Marcus. I can't believe I fell asleep and it's not even eleven yet."

"Hey, it's no problem. I will walk you in."

He guided her with his hand upon her waist up to her door. Before entering her apartment she looked up at Marcus and through the haze of her buzz she apologized.

"I feel terrible about drinking so much and this being a special celebration for you. It's unlike me to lose control like this. I'm so sorry Marcus." Valentina lowered her eyes in shame. Lifting her chin he noticed she kept her eyes cast down hiding tears that rimmed on the edge of her lashes. He bent down and kissed her cheek and inhaled to catch her elegant perfume.

"You never need to apologize. My night was special because you were there for me. May I help you inside?"

"Thank you for always being such a steady force in my life. I can always count on you. I'll take it from here."

"Okay, then sweet dreams. I'll see you tomorrow."

"See you. Oh and Marcus?" He had made a slight turn to walk away but stopped when she called."

"Yes Valentina."

"Congratulations." She gave him a small smile that filled him with expectation. This time he stood there as she entered the apartment and locked her door thinking how he wanted to hold her in his arms and kiss the sadness off her beautiful face.

The pitter-patter of the dog's nails against the dark mahogany flooring broke Valentina's uneasy sleep. She stretched out and recoiled her body as her little Jack Russell terrier Lola bounced on her abdomen. Nothing ever prepares one for the thud and sometimes-painful pounce of a four-legged friend. With regret she stopped playing with the sweet white and caramel colored dog and reluctantly dragged herself out of bed.

She had two hours to shower, dress, eat breakfast, feed and walk the dog before heading out to work and her head was heavy and fuzzy. The gray New York skies didn't help her mood lift either as she turned the coffee maker on and entered the cold bathroom with the floor to ceiling white subway tiles that gave the place a minimalist, barren appearance.

Valentina was tall with long, wavy, chestnut hair cascading beyond her shoulder blades. Her body was still youthful at 35 with long toned legs and arms and rounded breasts that showed her commitment three times a week to running and Pilates. She hated conventional exercise but was devoted to Pilates and its toning and firming of all muscle groups.

After dressing, she drank her coffee along with two aspirins, inhaled a 100-calorie sandwich thin with low fat cream cheese and quickly walked the sprite little dog around the block only stopping at State News to pick up a copy of The New York Times.

The Upper East Side was quiet at 6:30 in the morning. The only disturbances came from rattling garbage trucks barreling down the streets that rudely jolted people awake. Shouts coming from crude sanitation men hoisting bags of waste into cavernous voids added to the racket. The men stopped to stare at the beautiful, tall woman in black leggings tucked neatly into shiny designer black leather riding boots, as she exited the pre war doorman building. The windy day swirled her glossy hair around, as she regretted not wearing her hat. The camel colored Searle coat kept her warm but she hated the cold regardless of the efficiency of the expensive cashmere lining. Inside her black leather shoulder bag she tucked in the paper and rushed to the corner for a taxi. The traffic along 72nd street was picking up with small waves of yellow taxis readying to gather passengers.

Finding a cab was simple enough but traveling downtown to Broadway and 18th street was a test in patience. Valentina did not want to work today. Her mind was cloudy from too much champagne the night before at the awards ceremony. After she got home there had been no reason to justify more champagne but this was the only way she could numb her senses to what David shared when he called. She started and finished the bottle of Le Grand Dame by herself and cried into the early morning hours. Nothing could have prepared Valentina for her former boyfriend David's announcement of his sudden engagement to Diana Monroe.

Their relationship ended just three weeks prior but Valentina still loved him and thought they could get through this rough patch. Two years of being in a relationship that led to nothing but a broken heart required more than a bottle of champagne to ease the nerves. Even girlfriend intervention could not help with this disastrous news. Valentina felt very much alone with her problem.

To distract herself she opened up the paper and fumbled around until she found the neatly folded Lifestyle section. As the taxi moved and jerked along to the West Side and downtown area of Manhattan she glanced around the pages lazily. There it was in full view for her heart to break just a little more, the engagement announcement of Doctor David Harrington to socialite and philanthropist Diana Monroe. Valentina removed her sunglasses that hid already red and swollen eyes to read the announcement again. The attractive blond woman smiled sweetly at the camera with her left arm strategically hooked on David's elbow to display the substantial diamond ring.

Recognizing the blond from the night before at the awards ceremony Valentina recalled the woman sitting between Marcus and Mr. Woolsley without an idea as to who she was at the time. Thoughts invaded and tormented Valentina causing her to feel ill.

Why and how did this happen? What planet was I on to not know these two already knew each other? We just ended our thing three weeks ago and David is already engaged!

The cab arrived at Infinity Acquisitions at 900 Broadway. Her hurt was quickly becoming anger with a strong taste of bile rising from her stomach. The turbaned driver stopped the meter at $23.50. Quickly she handed over $25.00 and rushed out and welcomed the brisk wind and noisy sounds of traffic. She threw the Times into the corner waste bin and proceeded to enter the building.

Infinity Acquisitions sparkled with unique and exotic furnishings from around the globe. Countless number of shiny chandeliers of varying sizes and colored crystals illuminated the main floor like a box of jewels. It wasn't a cheesy and predictable import store but rather an elegant place of fine linens and furnishings. This 10-floor sanctum of privilege and style smelled exquisitely from the many aromas of incense, soaps and colognes that were displayed lavishly throughout. The beautiful warehouse housed expensive and unique collections with the purpose to create beauty and a sense of magic in every space. The retail half of the company was what all visitors saw but the part where Valentina worked in was in buying unique and one of a kind furnishings from auctions houses and estate sales. These furnishings and home decor were often reserved for the coveted few who could afford and desired antique or rare pieces.

Desperate to get to her office Valentina rushed over to the closing elevator doors. She pushed through with her bag and caused the doors to re-open. She stepped in and quickly scanned the faces before her and then quickly lowered what she was sure were tell tale eyes of a woman betrayed. The elevator was packed with several employees chatting and balancing briefcases along with Starbucks coffee cups. Valentina noticed her boss Marcus Napier standing to the far end of the elevator having his ear chewed off by Spencer Nolan, director of marketing.

"When was the last time you went golfing in Scotland, Napier?" Marcus heard Nolan but his mind was on the woman he desired more than anything. Valentina looked straight ahead into the highly polished stainless steel doors where she caught Marcus staring straight at her. Marcus looked away and responded to Nolan's inquiry, "Well, I have never golfed in Scotland. In fact, I haven't been back in decades. Sorry I can't help you with that one Nolan but last Spring I went a few rounds in the Bahamas." Nolan huffed at Napier's mention and added, "The Bahamas is good golf country but really you must get back to Scotland. It's incredible out there. Perhaps we can arrange a little excursion. Napier wanted to get his colleague off his back to move up closer to Valentina. "Sure thing Nolan. Whatever you want. See you around." Both men quickly affirmed farewells with a quick bow of their heads.

People moved out on varying floors. Nolan left on the third leaving Valentina, Marcus and two other people in the elevator. Moving up to her as the elevator emptied out he said casually, "Hi Valentina, feeling better?" Valentina looked up at the handsome man in the crisp suit and fresh Armani cologne. She always felt safe around Marcus because there was something about the extraordinary light and sincerity that his eyes gave off. The deep blue of his soulful eyes gave her the impression they were trying to tell her something very personal. She gave a tepid smile and said, "Oh, I'm fine Marcus and thanks again for taking me home last night."

"It was my pleasure. Are you sure you are alright?" Marcus whispered.

Keeping her head down she responded, "I guess. You know, LIFE. Sometimes it can be a real…problem."

Besides feeling safe with Marcus Valentina thought he was very handsome and felt an attraction to him but they worked together and he was her direct supervisor. She knew that she could lose her job if she ventured into such a situation. Her career mattered a great deal to her even if it meant putting soft feelings for Marcus to the side.

Their eyes met and he noticed how red rimmed they were and how her face wore a horrible mask of sorrow. Marcus could only guess that Valentina had already found out about her ex boyfriend and Diana Monroe.

The ding of the elevator bell rang for the fifth floor where they stepped off. Valentina rushed out to the left while Marcus stood there looking at her walk rapidly towards her office. She stopped midway and looked back to return another weak smile and noticed he was watching her as well. He continued to move along the opposite direction to his office and the multitude of meetings that were on his agenda.

The woman he loved was right under his thumb and he couldn't pursue her because company policy was strict about employees commingling. Too many years had passed and he was no longer willing to wait. For Marcus Napier front and center was Valentina and he had to tell her how he felt or he would go mad.

CHAPTER 2

Escape

Cece was already at her desk with mail, appointments and a venti caramel lite latte from Starbucks for Valentina. The cherubic faced twenty three year old assistant looked up to her elegant boss and knew from Valentina's expression and pallor that something terrible had happened.

Cece also understood that it was going to be a long and cold day. Valentina was usually bubbly, effervescent like her beloved champagne. Not much bothered the experienced buyer of international furnishings but this morning her demeanor showed tired, puffy eyes and a paleness unlike her usual healthy glow. Cece suspected it had to be because of David. She never liked the pompass ass that called the office and made brusque demands. Cece had his number from the beginning.

She felt a kinship with Valentina, as they were both girls from the Northeast Bronx. Valentina grew up in Pelham Bay and Cece in Castle Hill. Although Valentina had long ago moved into Manhattan and was a well traveled, sophisticated woman, Cece was just starting her career after graduating from Hunter College with a degree in education. After a part time job as a sales associate she realized that her passions were in estate acquisitions. Cece was petite and voluptuous with a generous bosom and an even more pronounced rear. She was a classic hourglass only quite small in stature. What she lacked in height she made up for in loyalty and efficiency. She traveled daily on the number 6 train from Castle Hill where she lived with her parents, grandmother and younger brother.

Becoming a buyer of fine furnishings for Infinity was her ultimate goal and she always felt she hit potluck when she was assigned to be Valentina's assistant. She had no shame in picking her boss's brain over furniture styles, history, fabrics and a milieu of industry related matters. The industry she worked in respected knowledge, experience and buyers who understood value. To Cece this opportunity was a way out of the noisy, overcrowded streets around her neighborhood. She longed to live in Manhattan but with the rentals being ten times what her parents paid in their $750.00 month, three bedroom rent controlled apartment, Cece understood all too well that saving her money made more sense. In a few years she could move out and be on her own. In the mean time, she soaked up everything she could from the knowledgeable people she worked with and dreamt of someday being a purveyor of fine furnishings and estates.

"Hi Cece, please cancel all appointments for today, thanks," said Valentina in a voice barely above a whisper.

"Okay, I'll be right outside if you need anything." Cece said softly as she closed the door and left Valentina slumped in her white leather office chair staring onto the surface of the glass desk. That cold feeling in her stomach had returned along with a stress induced right temple headache.

I need to just ride this wave, this too shall pass, and this too shall pass. Valentina rubbed her temples gently as she mumbled this to herself.

She tried not to think of that snake David with his handsome face and steely gray eyes. Contemplating at how much farther her life had unraveled with the engagement in the Times, tears pushed through to the surface and she let out her anguish. That newspaper announcement had Valentina in a near catatonic state unable to move and with complete confusion clouding her mind. The morning crawled along and she remained in the same position. By one p.m. Valentina wasn't too certain if she hadn't dozed off or fainted while sitting up. Her head kept spinning the same thoughts around and around.

He broke up with me and then gets engaged in fewer than three weeks to a socialite and I'm sitting here in a fog of confusion. Enough of this bullshit, David played me wrong and the entire time we were "together" he had this other girlfriend. Go to Hell." She shouted in her mind.

Her temples were throbbing but little by little Valentina was crawling out of this dense fog. With effort she lifted off the chair and walked slowly aware of new body aches she had never felt before. Reaching into her bag, which lay on the white, Italian leather sectional she rummaged through until she found Tylenol and took two with a sip of water. The latte was now cold but she felt her throat parched and drank it down.

"Cece, come in," called Valentina over the phone. She stretched out on the sofa with a bottle of water and rested her head against the palm of her hand. Cece walked in gingerly and sat across from her boss to wait patiently for instructions.

"Is the proposal for the Madrid job still available?" asked Valentina calmly and slowly. Cece watched her boss with trepidation because she knew she did not want to travel since her last trip to Bulgaria proved to be a waste of time.

"It's still open. No one has stepped up to claim it yet. Why?" asked Cece.

Valentina rubbed her temple and quickly responded, "Send Marcus an email and get me on the next flight out to Spain. Prepare all documentation for Lola because I'm not planning on rushing back which means she's coming and make certain it's first class and she goes on board with me," added Valentina.

Cece was shocked at her boss' sudden change of heart. With hesitation she added, "Okay, will do, but what about the jobs you have pending here? I mean this seems so sudden. Are you alright?"

Valentina looked up at the young assistant. She really liked Cece because she was quick, smart and opinionated. She felt like a big sister to the wide-eyed girl. Sitting up from her reclined position Valentina fought back tears as she explained to Cece. "If I don't get out of New York I will lose my mind. I threw out the paper but go on the New York Times site on your iPad and read the social announcements." Cece dutifully yet nervously clicked away until she found the announcement page. She read the page as Valentina watched her reaction. As expected her eyes widened and ruby painted mouth made an O shape. She looked at her boss and said in a brash manner, "The fuckin' douche bag! I knew he was a creep. The no good worthless piece of…" Valentina held her hand up and stopped Cece from expounding further expletives although she felt good hearing them directed towards David.

"So you understand why I need to get the Hell away to clear my head and recover some semblance of peace," explained Valentina.

It was hard for Cece to get what her boss was saying because the fighter in her wanted to skewer David but she relented and calmly said, "Alright, I will redirect all your other jobs and get these plans together. But seriously, you are running away and while I get that, I think you should contact that other chick and let her know she's engaged to an asshole." She got up but before she opened the door to leave she turned around and added, "Wanna do lunch, because you look busted and he's not worth it." Valentina chuckled at the honesty of her assistant and responded quickly, "Yes, let's do lunch."

Le Cuisine, the popular organic restaurant located in the store was crowded and buzzing with midday chatter.

They sat against the wall at a small table for two draped in starched white linens with heavy stainless steel cutlery. Breezing through the menu they knew well they ordered crispy shrimp romaine for Valentina and a spinach, goat cheese pizza for Cece. The conversation was all about David and how deceptive he was. Cece continued bashing David but after glancing at Valentina's solemn expression she mellowed out and let her speak. Valentina put down her fork and spoke with measured words. "What he did was wrong and I will never forgive him for deceiving me. In a way, I feel liberated because if he were this vile why would I want to find it out later? Better to know it now. I'm reeling from the hurt and lies but I'm not a fool to see how fortunate I am." Valentina made a deep sigh trying to believe her own words and took another sip of the crisp and refreshing Riesling. Cece raised both eyebrows and responded, "Yes, in a very logical world that is true but I want to rip his head off just the same. If this is how you can get over him then more power to you. But why do you want to go off to Spain? If you can see things so logically then why not stay where you are and go about your business? I have to stay here and deal with all those pompous jerks in the office and twiddle my thumbs until you get back! And God forbid I have to work with Darren, the wormy little creep. He's always trying to make a play on me."

Cece was right but in Valentina's heart the pain was raw and New York for all its glamour and parties is a very small town if you traveled in certain circles. She knew running away was a way of not facing what just happened but she also knew it was a way of cleansing her soul. She felt abused, used like a kitchen rag and thrown to the side. The difficult question that kept widening the hole in her heart was, what about her wasn't good enough for David Harrington? She was accomplished, educated, well traveled and attractive. In fact, she was often described at beautiful with classical features, statuesque, willowy and strong. All she lacked was a family of her own and at 35 the clock wasn't ticking it was blaring loudly. She looked into Cece's very young inexperienced eyes and wondered if the girl could ever understand her motives.

Leaving for a month or so was therapeutic and she would keep busy working on acquiring and establishing provenance on the contents of an apartment in an exclusive neighborhood in Madrid. All Valentina knew about this job was the name of the housekeeper and that this had been the residence of a deceased duchess. Infinity Acquisitions knew it housed some Art Deco lamps, tables and sconces that were period pieces, expensive and supposedly genuine. Valentina had to work with the auction house in Madrid to negotiate deals and move the pieces of interest to her company. Spain was an obvious choice because she spoke the language fluently and felt at home in the large, noisy and busy metropolis of Madrid.

Valentina laughed at Cece's dramatic expressions and added, "So perhaps I can figure a way for you to come along once I know what's happening over there. Lauren travels with her boss quite a lot. Perhaps you can too. No promises but I will try."

Cece leapt from her chair and hugged her boss taking in the expensive and delicious Tom Ford fragrance that was everywhere on her person. They giggled and genuinely liked one another, which made this difficult day so much easier to cope with. After lunch, the women decided on a walk around the block to help digestion and chat a bit more and then headed back to the office.

CHAPTER 3

Suddenly

While Cece finalized all the preparations for Valentina's upcoming trip, Valentina headed straight to Marcus Napier's office and asked his secretary Melanie for a word with him. The stoic woman escorted her into the enormous corner office with mid century burl wood furnishings and leather chairs and sofas. His massive desk was made of maple wood with elegant carved lion feet polished to a subtle sheen. To her surprise the tall, slender man lifted from his chair and came around and gave her a gentle hug.

Marcus Napier was a man of calculating taste. He was as precise about his bespoke Brioni suits as he was about his furnishings. Twenty years as head of the acquisitions department for such a prestigious company spoke volumes to his professional and discriminating taste. He invited her to sit down on one of two forest green leather chairs. Valentina always ran her thumb and index fingers along the nail heads on the armrests. The sensation was cool, hard and gave her a sense of the masculinity of the space and the man. Being in his office was one of her favorite things about working at Infinity. She inhaled the aroma of Armani classic fragrance as it gently permeated everywhere in the elegant office.

Marcus went right to the point, "I read the email that you are taking the Spain job. Why the change of heart when you were all set for the Connecticut and Long Island estate acquisitions?"

Valentina didn't want her boss to know she was running away to help heal a broken heart. She lied and carefully danced around the issue. "I wanted to return to Europe to set up this deal. You know how much I enjoy a mystery and this apartment contains deco pieces. It's too exciting to pass up," Valentina smiled showing her perfectly aligned teeth.

She knew Marcus had certain feelings for her and she respectfully kept her distance because they worked together but given the opportunity she would entertain the idea. Valentina liked how he was especially gallant towards her at auctions and charities they attended as employees of Infinity. He always escorted her back to her building and never missed an opportunity at complimenting her work. But today she noticed just how deeply he cared for her as his eyes seared hers.

Marcus came around and sat by her side and spoke softly, "I can then assume you aren't running away from David Harrington and his engagement announcement." Valentina blushed and she knew he saw her cheeks burn a crimson color. Realizing he knew everything, she had no other recourse but to be honest.

"Yes, it is true we are no longer together but my reasons for going to Spain are in the best interest of the company and have nothing to do with my personal life or previous relationship," she added quickly in a slightly curt tone that tinged the atmosphere with tension.

Marcus realized he had hit a nerve and quickly went to remediate the indiscretion, "Your ex doesn't realize that his loss is another man's gain. You are a diamond Valentina. Go to Spain, do the work and clear your head. You have my blessings." He got up and extended his hand to offer it to her.

She willingly took it and let it linger in his. Marcus had all the chivalry a girl could ever want. This worldly sophisticated man fascinated her. He closed his hand tighter around hers and said, "Be careful over there and I hope the change will help you leave New York behind for a short while. By the time you return this will be old news. A change of air will do you good." He brought her hand up to meet his lips as he planted a kiss.

Valentina felt her cheeks grow hot and a stirring in her stomach she had never felt before until now. She looked closely at the tall, handsome man standing before her and noticed for the first time the slight hints of sparkling silver that graciously adorned his temples and how the full head of polished and styled hair was a deep brown with flecks of silver peeping throughout. The deep blue of his eyes surprised her and made her take a step back. Those same expressive eyes caught her off guard and were sending a different message. She was confused and feeling a bit dizzy. Hurriedly she spoke as she made her way to the door, "Thank you Marcus, I will call you when I have some news on the job." He nodded and watched her turn the knob and walk out of his office and his life once again.

Walking back to the window Marcus took out a Dunhill and inhaled deeply. He often thought about how he was 45 and was 10 years her senior. All her former boyfriends were young men around her age. He wondered if she would consider giving a wiser, more mature man the slightest chance. To Marcus she was the full package and too often he watched her get her heart mangled in the hands of foolish men. All he could do was let her have the jobs that helped her run away and recuperate enough for the next man to come and hurt her all over again.

When she started at Infinity Acquisitions eleven years ago, she was young, and bubbly. Always smiling and with an infectious laugh that made Marcus relax in her presence.

Back then she was his assistant and rose up the ranks until she became a certified and skilled buyer. He was her mentor and she a very apt student. Unfortunately for Marcus he knew her suitors all too well since she started working as his assistant.

There was the assistant professor from Hunter College. He was a young, brash, man with a messy head of hair. Not sophisticated in the least but she found something in him that he could not imagine what it could be. Then there was the Peugeot dealership owner from Queens. He wore a pinky ring and Marcus wanted to punch him when he found Valentina sniffling one morning in her office after she discovered he was also dating her friend.

Two years ago, she started dating Dr. David Harrington a young, handsome, polished orthopedic surgeon at Lenox Hospital. All signs would indicate he was a great match for her but like the others he put Valentina last to his needs.

Marcus let out a long intake of smoke and just could not understand what it was about those men Valentina found so interesting when one after the other betrayed her. He would never do this to her because all he thought about was loving her and making her laugh again like she once did eleven years ago when he first met the young, creative woman.

When he met Valentina, Marcus was married. His wife had been diagnosed with advanced bone marrow cancer. Marcus fought along with her and was committed to the end but after 12 years together his wife died in his arms at Beth Israel hospital and since then he had devoted his life to his work and to admiring Valentina from afar. At 45, a widower and collector of art he lived in a quiet, elegant world of beautiful things and people that stifled him. Although respected by members of his social circles and sought after as a suitor nothing filled his soul.

If Valentina ever felt something for him he or she would have to leave Infinity and pursue careers elsewhere. Leaving was of no concern to him but he would only walk away if he knew Valentina had feelings for him as well. He knew that to Valentina he was just this older guy who was her former mentor and the director of acquisitions with a healthy share of company stock and wealthy in his own right. He lit another cigarette and reluctantly directed his attention to his work as Valentina filled his heart with longing and desire.

By early afternoon it was impossible for Marcus to work as Valentina's brown suede eyes continuously flashed before his mind. He threw down the papers he held and paced around the office thinking that if only she felt something for him he would leave and they could pursue a relationship. For her, he would leave it all behind. The muscles in his jaw twitched and he knew it was not a good sign because it told him he was getting restless with pretending. Marcus Napier was not good at pretending. He was direct and precise. He knew he had to act quickly before she met someone else who would steal her away from him and this time perhaps for good.

CHAPTER 4

Clear the Decks

Valentina rushed pass Cece and into her office after her exchange with Marcus. She stood before her desk and stared out onto 18th street. The street was busy with people and cars. She watched a young man maneuver a bike into Sports Authority and thought about what just happened with Marcus. She had had countless conversations with the man, done the lunch, dinner, cocktail parties but always as associates for the company. It was Marcus who several years ago put her in contact with the right realtor that helped her find the two bedroom, two-bath gem on the Upper East Side around the corner from her alma mater, Marymount Manhattan College. She thought of how he treated her with extreme care, gentle manners, respect and affection.

There it was, she thought. *Marcus doesn't like me, it's way more than that. Oh my God! All this is way too much.* She concluded.

By three p.m. she had decided that all this drama was enough for one day. She collected her bag, grabbed her coat and pulled it on through her arms hurriedly. As she headed out the door, Cece handed her the boarding pass for the trip to Spain and all other documentations. Cece was so busy talking about how she prepped everything that she had not noticed the look of confusion and restlessness in Valentina's eyes.

"Oh and I have you booked at the AC Palacio del Retiro. They take dogs and there's this big old park and," Cece stopped talking when she finally noticed Valentina's blank expression.

Valentina hugged and thanked her assistant while saying, "Cece, I am nothing without you. I won't be in tomorrow to get myself ready and close the apartment so I will call you Thursday from Madrid. I'm going home." Cece was surprised, as her boss never left work before six p.m. and it was only around three in the afternoon. She figured that given the craziness of the day it was only normal for Valentina to go relax and get ready for a trip that might take several weeks.

"Okay, safe trip and don't forget you will need me over there as your assistant, hint, hint," teased Cece. It never failed; Cece always helped Valentina step out of her head if just for a second.

"Don't worry, I won't forget. Give me a week to establish our position over there. Take care Cece and thanks for everything."

Cece beamed, "No sweat, I will look forward to hearing from you." Both women hugged once again and Valentina grabbed her files, left the office and dashed past the front entrance of the busy store. She hailed a cab and headed home.

In the cab she flipped over the Madrid job file and quickly committed the name of the estate to memory and stuffed the file into her bag. She took out another file and told herself not to think about Marcus and those blue eyes of his or how he held her hand longer and tighter than usual. She usually saw nothing more than admiration from a mentor to a mentee. But Valentina could not fool herself because the message his eyes conveyed was of longing and desire, not pride. She shook her head in an attempt to erase Marcus out of her mind and paid the cab.

Antonio her doorman held open the door for her, "Good afternoon Ms. Puig. Oh, you have a delivery. I will bring it up for you because it is heavy." Valentina looked around the lobby and saw no boxes, "What delivery Antonio? I'm not expecting packages."

The pudgy but smartly uniformed doorman with a neat mustache quickly directed her attention to the impressive arrangement of lilies, trilliums and roses, in a large rectangular glass vase. Valentina wondered who they could be from and noticed the flowers were from her favorite florist, Fellan and Co. She pulled from a crisp white envelope with her full name written in ink a tiny pink card. In Marcus' neat handwriting it read, *Come back when you are ready, I will be here waiting for you. Regards, Marcus.*

Valentina stared at the name and looked up nonchalantly at her doorman and smiled. Antonio quickly picked up the arrangement and proceeded to the elevator. At her door, a very enthusiastic Lola met Valentina. "Just leave them on this table please and thank you Antonio." Lola barked at the doorman and jumped around happily to see Valentina. She handed him a folded $10.00 bill which he politely and promptly refused and locked the door behind her.

Immediately without allowing herself to ponder over the message she lifted Lola and kissed her honey colored cheeks, changed her clothes into running gear, grabbed the leash, keys and ran out. Once outside she felt the cold hit her harder with just her dry wick jacket, long sleeve tee shirt and running pants. But the cold was exactly what she needed to numb her senses from the drama of the day.

"Let's go for a walk Lola and then a nice run along the park," she said calmly. The beautiful little dog pranced about and wiggled her bottom as Valentina walked up the block heading west towards Central Park. She walked quickly but paused enough times to give the dog a chance to sniff and mark her spot. They jogged in unison along Fifth Avenue and entered the park where the city disappeared. Valentina loved this park and being here with Lola. She threw out in a large green garbage bin Lola's waste and proceeded to run over forty minutes together. The air was crisp and cold but it didn't matter to them once their bodies warmed up. They ran along the Mall, past the famous Dakota building along Central Park West looped half way around the Great Lawn and down by the Jackie Kennedy Onassis Reservoir until they reached 72nd street and walked home the rest of the way to regulate their hearts. Running and Pilates helped her clear her head. The cobwebs that had dulled her mind earlier were gone. David was a bullet she averted but his betrayal still stung and hurt deeply thus making this wound too fresh for her to dismiss.

Valentina ran down the day in her head. It was a habit she had since she was young and shared with her parents what she had done in school. She remembered how she awoke with a headache followed by humiliation and a greater heartache. Marcus kissed her hand and squeezed a little life back into her and finally surprised her with an insanely expensive and gorgeous arrangement of flowers. All she had left to do was to get home, shower and relax.

Once home, she wiped down Lola and inspected her paws for any tears. This dog was the child she never had and all those maternal instincts needing an escape were flourished on the pretty pup. She fed Lola, made some tea, lit a few candles along her large tub and added some fragranced oils. She stepped into the shower where she scrubbed the distress away and washed her long hair. Lola was lounging by the tub waiting, as was her habit. The little dog with the almond shaped eyes loved Valentina without measure and the feeling was mutual. They were always together and loved each other's company.

The warmth of the water relaxed her aching muscles and gave way for tears to flow. She cried for time lost on David, for broken promises, for being humiliated and embarrassed in such a public manner. Big heavy tears fell because she knew everyone would have seen that announcement in the Times, and because she was 35 and the only family she had was her aunt in the Bronx and her little Lola.

After a good cry she sipped her now cooled tea and patted herself down gently. All day she had avoided her twenty-six text messages and fourteen calls. The phone was still on silent and it would remain this way until tomorrow or the next day. There were more important things to do than regurgitate the David story and although her friends were important to her she was not in the mood to talk. She was thankful for not having a Facebook or Twitter account as this relationship mess would have been all over these social outlets and the last thing Valentina ever wanted was to be on anyone's lips as gossip.

Sleep came quickly, deeply and gratefully. No signs of David floated about in her head. It was Marcus and his handsome distinguished face that did emerge at one point but it wasn't a nightmare instead it felt more like a warm, gentle breeze caressing her skin. Valentina smiled in her sleep and Lola snored softly next to her.

CHAPTER 5

Melancholy

Wednesday morning was brisk, cold and sunny. Thankfully the sun made the cold seem less dreary and gave the day a sense of freshness. Valentina woke up energetic and after her regular morning duties of feeding and walking the dog, she walked down to 68th and 2nd Avenue to the Veterinarians office.

The overweight receptionist wearing a blue smock and pants with a repeating dog bone pattern that were two sizes too tight asked with enthusiasm, "Hi, welcome to East Side Vets. What can I help you with?" Valentina thought to herself how the girl sounded like a recording. She quickly explained her flight needs and the receptionist looked up Lola's file on the computer.

"Oh sure, Lola is up to date with all her shots so we can issue a clearance letter in about 1 hour. The cost is $50.00." Valentina quickly paid for the letter and told the woman she would return in one hour. She went over to Duane Reade and picked up fresh Alka seltzer tablets along with more band-aids and Neosporin. There were bottles of Aleve and Tylenol still good from the last trip. She was an experienced traveler and knew these items to be priceless when one was abroad and sick.

Back at the vets she picked up the letter and dashed home where she threw these purchases into her carryon bag and the letter into the zippered compartment. She thought about what she could be forgetting and remembered the Children's Benadryl for Lola. Half a teaspoon before they board and the pup would sleep calmly rather than get all jumpy and yappy over the engine noise and unfamiliar surroundings. She took out Lola's carry bag and placed a fresh wee wee pad over the upholstered flooring along with her blanket and toy. The pockets were stuffed with more pads and a sweater. Valentina figured she would need thirty wet food trays and packed those in the mesh compartment of her suitcase along with 4 gallon sized bags of dry dog food. Lola was set.

Now she had to pack for herself. This was easy. One pair of boot leg jeans, two Ponte skinny pants one black, one burgundy, one sheath black dress, several scarves, blouses, two thin cashmere sweaters, her Thinsulate black short raincoat, two sets of running gear, sports bra, underwear sets two nudes, two black, one pair of dress shoes, her thigh high new Prada boots, one pair of ballet flats and her running shoes. Several pieces of jewelry, fragrance, skincare, shampoo, conditioner and makeup in full sizes because it would be at least one month. She would wear her cashmere camel coat, gloves and pack a hat as well. She knew how to mix and match classic pieces together and always looked like she packed up the entire closet. The last thing to do was get her passport out of the safe in the back of her closet where she kept all her expensive jewelry and documents. Valentina had a rule, never travel with anything that had to be insured.

She sat down to write a note to her housekeeper, Josefa, who came every Monday and Friday. In the envelope she left the cleaning woman instructions and money to pick up her dry cleaning next Tuesday, throw out all the food in the fridge unless she wanted to take it home for her family and a list of what to buy before her arrival one month later.

By mid afternoon she was exhausted. She made a kale and tuna salad and sat down to munch on this with a glass of Riesling. She kicked off her Nikes and curled up on her sofa with Lola by her side and the phone in her hand. She started playing her messages. Three friends left calls regarding the article, another left ideas for revenge, her aunt in the Bronx called about some distant relative being sick and then there was David's call.

She heard the voicemail, "Hi Vale, just calling to tell you how sorry I am that things ended the way they did. I just didn't want you to be surprised by the announcement in the Times. You are very special and I do love you…"

Valentina stopped the message and erased it. She sent him a quick text,

Lose my number, I NEVER want to hear from you again.

She took a deep breath as her finger pressed the send button. She read the remaining texts and as expected they were all about the same announcement. Everyone shared their shock and feigned concern. She erased and cleared all her messages and texts from the iPhone. To ease the concern of her three closest friends who had called she sent out a group text and informed them about her upcoming trip to Madrid and how she was so over David. She promised to do lunch when she returned but was getting ready for the trip and had no time to chat or text. The only person she did call was her Tía Carmela.

Carmela Suarez was 65 years young. She lived alone in a one bedroom cooperative apartment, exercised three times per week at L.A. Fitness and did all her own cooking and shopping. She organized dances and taught tango at the senior center. The sprite woman drove around in her 2007 Jetta Volkswagon and never missed mass on Sundays. While Carmela never married she did not lack suitors. Like Valentina she was tall, slender and wore her hair in a classic silver haired bob. She wore tortoise shell glasses and never left her house looking undone. Carmela was brought up to always look polished regardless of what she was doing. A woman always had her face, hair and hands done. Clothing had to be clean and pressed. She retired after 25 years as a public school teacher in Brooklyn where she taught Spanish to mostly reluctant High School students. Although her pension was enough for a good life she measured her money carefully and took occasional trips to Florida and cruises with other retired friends. Carmela was a voracious reader in both languages and enjoyed painting. On many occasions she looked after Lola when Valentina went on short trips but the energy of the little Jack Russell proved to be too much for Carmela for trips extending beyond a week.

Valentina called her aunts landline. No answer. No surprise there as Carmela was rarely home. She tried her cell phone and a bright hello came across the line.

"Querida, how are you?" chirped Carmela.

"Hi Tía, I'm fine, just calling to let you know that I did get your message about cousin Alfredo and also to tell you that I am leaving to work in Madrid for about one month."

Valentina hoped Carmela would not ask her about David but that was just wishful thinking. "Vale, what about David? You cannot leave your handsome novio alone like that for so long. Some other woman can come along and snatch him up!" She had a hearty laugh but when her niece did not respond she knew something was wrong.

"Qué pasa?"

Valentina took a deep breath and told her aunt what had happened including the engagement announcement. A quiet, "Díos mio, lo siento querida," was heard from Carmela.

"Thanks Tía, but better I know who he is now than later on." Valentina added with a phony chirpiness to her voice. Her aunt retorted, "Oh of course m'ija, men, you never can be certain. But you know you must stand tall, proud and keep moving forward. He has no idea what he just lost, estupido."

It was always good to talk to her only immediate relative. Her aunt was strong and had a, *"don't let them see you sweat,"* attitude that had served her well throughout her life.

Valentina was raised by her mother Amalia and Carmela after her father died from a heart attack. Hernando Puig was a friendly, portly man with a boisterous laugh and a habit of slapping people roughy on their backs when he said hello. He was an importer of Spanish food products and loved food and wine. No one matched Hernando when it came to drinking his Rioja and eating.

Like most immigrants, he came to America with hopes and dreams but his were short lived. He adored his wife and little girl and they lacked for nothing. The home was always filled with food, music, laughter, family and friends. Valentina remembered impromptu parties and dinners that had as a central theme the celebration of life.

When Valentina was seven years old she heard her mother scream in the kitchen and ran out to see her father collapsed on the floor. A milieu of neighbors, and other people filled their small apartment in the Bronx as police and an ambulance took her father away. Her Tía Carmela arrived that evening and wrapped both her sister Amalia and Valentina in her arms and stayed until Valentina moved out years later.

While Valentina was in her last year at college, Amalia developed uterine cancer. It was a stage four prognosis. By the time Valentina's graduation came around in May her mother was too weak to attend but her aunt Carmela attended and represented both parents. By mid August, Amalia lost her fight with the disease and shortly thereafter, Valentina moved away to her first apartment in a roach infested studio in Chinatown.

The conversation was nearing its end and Valentina as well as Carmela needed to say goodbye. Carmela spoke softly, "Be careful in your travels and call me anytime when you want to talk. I will always be here for you."

It was difficult not to let the tears flow so Valentina didn't try. Her voice became hoarse as she added, "I just want my own family. Both my parents are gone and I would like a child someday but I just come across these jerks who end up hurting me in the end." She sobbed to her aunt and Carmela just let her talk and controlled her own emotions. "Why did he leave me for that woman? Is she prettier, NO, but she has money and David is very ambitious. I'm just so tired of this scene and I want someone who will really treasure me for who I am," sobbed Valentina into the phone.

Carmela sighed and measured her words to help ease her nieces sorrow, "You know, we cannot choose our parents or family but we can be as selective as we want to be about whom we share our personal lives with. Don't be too picky or you will end up an old lady like me with no husband. But be more demanding, never settle and no more tears. He's not worth it, querida. Set your sights on a brighter future and a new possibility. Forget this clown."

Valentina sniffled quietly saying, "I know Tía, I know. I am going to continue getting ready for this work trip. I really did not want to travel but I feel I need to get out of town for a while. You know, until the dust settles."

"Enjoy Madrid, it's a fascinating city. You haven't been there in a while. Perhaps you can visit Barcelona where our family is from. I have fond memories myself. Where is Lolita staying?"

"She's coming with me, a month is too long to be without each other. Barcelona would be a nice side trip especially since it's coastal and Lola loves the beach. Bueno Tía, take care and I will call you when I return," responded Valentina who was now anxious to get off the phone.

"Bendición querida, and remember no more tears. Valla con Díos." Valentina clicked the phone with a quiet, "Adíos," as well.

Valentina checked her text messages and her friends all responded with,

Have a safe trip and call when you get back. Love, Rocio
Bring back a sexy Spaniard! XOXO, Lauren
You go girl! Oh and do me a favor and check out the Hermes store in Madrid. I need the pink croc Birkin and they are all out in Paris and Brussels. I'll wire you the money. Love, Lindsey

Rolling her eyes at her friends ridiculous desire to own a bag worth nearly $100,000 she threw the phone on the bed and curled up next to Lola and stroked her back. The playful pup turned on her back and exposed her belly, which Valentina immediately rubbed while making figure eights with her index finger. The puppy was delirious with joy and she felt herself calming down and thinking of Marcus. She did like Marcus but never entertained the idea of him as a possible candidate. He was her former mentor, her current boss, the header at all the big meetings in her department and the guy she or someone else in the office accompanied to Christie's or Sotheby's for an auction or a cocktail party.

In thinking about him as a man he always came up as this slightly older man who was very quiet, smart, polished, calculating, rich and extremely gentlemanly. Never before had she considered the possibility of giving Marcus Napier a chance even if she secretly found him to be handsome and somewhat smolderingly sexy.

Valentina thought of the times she had gone out with Marcus and did not recall ever feeling anything other than a work relationship between the two. She remembered a time she was withdrawn because a former boyfriend betrayed her with a girlfriend and she was sick to her stomach over the whole thing. Marcus went out of his way to comfort her by having lunch brought to her office and insisting she leave early. And the next day he made it a point to come speak with her personally and ask how she felt. But Valentina just chalked this up to Marcus being a really nice man and nothing more. But now she realized that perhaps she had been so absorbed with her own issues that she never took notice that Marcus was attentive and caring because he had feelings for her.

Lifting herself off the bed with Lola following closely at her heels she walked over to the foyer and looked at the stunning flowers. Her finger caressed a lily as her eyes took in the entire arrangement and she felt this desire to just hear his voice and share how much she loved the flowers. She wondered as she took in the gentle fragrances of the flowers if calling him would make her seem too interested. Then she figured a text would be a bit detached and cold. Deciding to call she walked back into the bedroom, picked up her phone and speed dialed his office number and extension.

Melanie's very professional voice responded, "Mr. Marcus Napier's office, how may I assist you?" Valentina calmy said, "Hi, Melanie it's Valentina, is Marcus available?"

"Hello Valentina, actually he's gone for the day, would you like to leave a message?" asked Melanie

"No, it's okay, I will call him from abroad. Thanks."

"Bye now and safe trip," clipped Melanie

She threw the phone again on the bed, walked around the room and decided to just thank Marcus when she saw him the next time. Calling his personal cell number was too much for her right now because all she could see was the love in his sapphire eyes and she wasn't certain she could handle anymore at this time.

CHAPTER 6

The Kiss

She is only about thirteen blocks away, ten blocks downtown and three cross-town. I can get to her immediately and tell her what she means to me or risk someone else stepping in my place. My place? Valentina doesn't even know I'm alive. That changes today.

Marcus ruminated throughout the ground floor of his townhouse on 82nd between 5th and Madison. He left work early and had the driver drop him off by her building. He stared at it from across the street and left when he started to feel like a stalker. From there he walked to his home and got into workout gear and went to his personal gym, which was just off the kitchen on the first floor. He built up a sweat to stage three of P90X. For a man of 45 his body looked young, virile and strong. When his wife died he took up working out to help release the grief and loneliness that typically accompanied losing a loved one. He felt better, lost some fat around the middle and two pant sizes. For the past eleven years he maintained a solid and lean size 34 pants and 42 jacket. Marcus enjoyed good food, wine and well tailored clothing. Being slim enabled him to wear anything he wanted. He always looked fashionable and polished.

Despite a comfortable and indulgent lifestyle, Marcus realized that what he truly desired always slipped from his grasp. Valentina was the only woman he wanted, needed and was determined to have. He finished his workout and drank down two bottles of Poland Spring water. Drying off the perspiration with his New York Yankees towel, he picked up his phone and dialed her number. The phone rang three times before she picked up.

"Hello?" Valentina saw who it was on the caller I.D. but she pretended anyway, not knowing exactly why she did this.

Marcus cleared his throat trying to sound casual, "Valentina." He said nothing else as if her name were a prayer. She could hear his steady breathing on the other end and asked, "Marcus, are you alright?"

Marcus became anxious and shook his head as he realized how nervous he felt.

"Valentina, I wanted to know if you received the flowers," he added quickly.

Feeling the blush of embarrassment rising up to her cheeks for her poor manners she rushed on, "Oh yes and they are gorgeous! Thank you so much. I called your line at work today but Melanie told me you had left."

Marcus cleared his throat again adding, "Glad to know you like the flowers. Are you all packed for Spain?"

"Yes, all set to go," she hated small talk and wanted either to get off the phone or for Marcus to say something of importance.

"Well, um, it's only seven, if you haven't had dinner yet, would you care to join me?" He felt his pulse pounding on the inside of his wrist. Marcus was always cool but this was unsettling for him. He needed to tell her how he felt but wasn't certain this was the right time. He was concerned he might scare her away so soon after an embarrassing break up. Yet he also did not want to be in the pathetic position as rebound man either. His mind was in turmoil and the way his body responded whenever he was in her presence or when hearing her voice did not help him think clearly.

Valentina took a deep breath. She figured it was only dinner. She always liked his company and concluded that a few hours with a man she admired and who lavished her with attention wasn't such a bad deal.

"Sure, give me an hour to get ready."

He paced around his gym rubbing his hand over his hair several times and finally looked out the window and said confidently, "I will pick you up at eight, it's casual." He said the casual part thinking it seemed more relaxing.

"Okay, sure thing. See you then, Oh, my address is…Oh never mind. You were here a just two nights ago." Valentina felt foolish.

The hearty rumble of his chuckle cut her off, "Yes, I know where you live. See you soon."

"Of course, how silly of me, see you in an hour." She pressed END and plugged in her phone because the battery was low as she made a mental note to pack the phone charger.

She turned around and saw herself in the full-length mirror. She approached the mirror as if she didn't recognize the woman looking back at her.

What am I doing? Going out to dinner with Marcus Napier my boss. There's no function… Okay dummy, whatever, go shower, get casual it's easy peesy. No high heels, just a sweater, jeans and boots.

Valentina showered, smoothed body oil generously all over and sprayed Neroli Portofino by Tom Ford. She walked into her spacious closet and sat in front of her pretty vanity with a round beveled mirror. She put on a matching black with pink lace bra and panty set, slipped into a pair of skinny Seven For All Mankind jeans, a loose Michael Kors waffle weave ivory cashmere sweater and her favorite comfortable pair of Ralph Lauren knee high boots. She dazzled the look up with her favorite Dior pink gloss, some mascara and a little dab of Nars Orgasm blush on the apple of each cheek. She turned her head over and brushed the long rich chocolate tresses until they gleamed. Throwing her hair back she allowed her natural center part to happen and just smoothed down a few strays with her fingers. She followed this with some gold hoops, sprayed a little more cologne and walked over to her full- length mirror.

Lola was lounging on the bed watching this ritual and glanced up eagerly at Valentina. Admiring herself closely she turned to Lola and asked playfully, "Not bad for 35 right muñeca?" The puppy responded by wagging her tail like a battery-powered toy.

The buzzer rang and she knew Marcus was downstairs. She picked up the phone and told the concierge to let him come up. Her apartment was neat, clean and very stylish. Everything about it screamed Valentina, from the deco lamps and sconces to the mirrored furniture scattered around the living room and her bedroom. The floors were of large plank hardwood mahogany and the walls were a soft dove gray color that helped the satin white of the paneled doors, baseboards and ceilings to stand out. Chandeliers added sparkle over the varying shades of whites, grays and silver on the sofa, pillows and chairs. All the furniture was of simple clean lines allowing the mirrors and light to express themselve. Sheer, silky, white curtains puddled to the floors. Valentina's space was easy glamour, neat and sparkly.

Her doorbell chimed and she confidently went forth to open it. Shock registered on her face when she saw Marcus' casual outfit because he never dressed in anything but a perfect suit and tie. He stood before her in clean and neat Levis, black boots, a black wool turtleneck and a navy pea coat.

"Aren't you going to ask me in?" He asked with a smirk, no longer feeling nervous. Seeing his dream before him and so close boosted his confidence.

She blushed and was certain her cheeks looked like she had been slapped. "Of course, do come in, I just never saw you dress in anything other than a suit and tie. You do casual very well," she giggled nervously.

He really is so good looking. Hmm, how did I not see him before? Valentina thought to herself as she discreetly scanned Marcus from top to bottom.

"Thank you and as usual you look stunning," Marcus added softly and looked at her with those intense blue eyes that pierced right through her heart and made fluttery spasms happen down below her navel. "Thank you Marcus," Valentina looked away shyly.

She added a little nervously realizing she sounded like a young girl, "See, I placed your flowers here." She pointed to the flowers as Lola came barreling across the apartment to bark at the stranger.

Valentina tried to hush her but Lola was determined to let this stranger know he was in her house and she had to be certain it was okay for him to be there. Marcus squatted to meet the small dog at her level and caressed her snout with his hand, calming the pup until her tail was wagging happily. She proceeded to sniff his boots and jeans and when she was tired she sat on her haunches and stared at him with her head cocked to the side. Marcus chuckled at how perceptive the little dog was and looked up and caught Valentina admiring him with a look in her eyes he had never seen before. While he and Lola were becoming acquainted she was watching closely. Marcus was indeed very handsome, poised and gentle and Valentina appreciated that he was kind to her dog. He was quickly making a place in her heart, as David was becoming a faded memory.

She invited him into the living room where she took his coat and asked him to sit down. He recognized the magnificent cool blue hand woven silk rug from Pakistan the store sold some years ago. Everything about her space was soft, calm and very chic. Over the tiny wall speakers, Lester Young played his sax to "Almost like being In Love." Marcus felt at home in the beautiful space with the tasteful furnishings, lighting and music. He secretly wished he didn't have to leave. Casually he called out to Valentina who was in the kitchen preparing cocktails and asked, "You like jazz music?"

"Oh sure," she called in return, "I grew up listening to a lot of jazz. My dad loved it and when he passed away my mom would play all his records to remember him." She handed him his favorite cocktail, a vodka gimlet with Rose's lime juice on the rocks. His eyebrows furrowed in surprise at this gesture and inquired, "How did you know?"

Valentina laughed softly as she held her wine glass with a refreshing Riesling, "Seriously, eleven years of working, traveling and going places with you and you always order a vodka gimlet. Why, I'm as perceptive as Lola." They laughed easily and looked affectionately at one another.

Impressed, he took a sip, shook his head approvingly and said, "Well, you always surprise me Valentina, this is the best vodka gimlet I have ever had." Again she felt her cheeks burn and looked away shyly. He took her hand in his and softly said, "We have reservations in a half hour at La Mirabelle, unless you prefer elsewhere."

Valentina loved the French provincial and quiet atmosphere at this restaurant. It was a place for people who appreciated home style Provence cooking.

"That sounds perfect to me. It's eight thirty now, shall we get going?" Valentina asked with a smile.

He stood up, placed his half consumed cocktail next to her barely touched wine. They walked to the hall closet where she handed him his coat and he helped her with the red Valentino hooded cape she wanted to wear. She placed her leather gloves on but before taking her bag she held up Lola and kissed her sweetly on the cheeks. Lola responded with a feverish wagging of her tail. Marcus took the opportunity that the puppy was eye level to rub the top of her head and tell her she's beautiful while looking at Valentina. This did not escape

Valentina in the least and when their eyes met she quickly looked away, placed Lola on the floor and opened her door.

The cold November night made Valentina shudder as she felt the sting on her cheeks. They quickly climbed into the backseat of the Audi and headed to the corner of West 86th street. Other than fleets of yellow cabs the streets were quiet. The car arrived in little time and during the entire short ride Marcus and Valentina did not look or talk to one another. She wondered if it was because he did not want his driver Jimmy to know his business. He wondered if she was uncomfortable around him outside of work encounters.

Jimmy Knowles, his driver of over fifteen years, was a small statured man who worshiped his boss. Marcus took care of those in his service and Jimmy never forgot how Marcus and the late Mrs. Napier paid for his sons medical bills when the boy was pummeled during football practice and went down with a concussion. Jimmy was a grateful man and though his son recovered he felt forever indebted to Marcus. Since that incident Marcus decided to pay his driver and housekeeper monthly medical premiums, help them set up IRA's for retirement while matching dollar for dollar their contributions.

Marcus was generous, as he understood about struggle. His childhood was one of poverty on the upper West Side. His parents were Scottish immigrants of little means. His father worked on the docks painting ships for the U.S. lines. Napier Sr. was a big and burly man but after one too many punches to the head in his youth attempting to become a boxer he had difficulty remembering details and sometimes had a lost look in his eyes. It was his mother Teresa who kept the family afloat with two jobs. The main job was as a cleaning woman in office buildings from four in the afternoon until midnight and during the day while Marcus was at school she cleaned the homes of wealthy people along Riverside and Central Park West They lived just off 91st and Amsterdam in a housing project that had just been built right along side posh, expensive condominium buildings and across the street from the tony Trinity school. During his childhood, Marcus spent countless afternoons running and playing up and down the streets from Riverside Park up to Central Park West. He played War with his group of friends that read like a League of Nations roster. In this little posse there were Italian's, Irish, Dominican's, African American's, Puerto Rican's and Jews. Together they were one as they hid in stairwells and behind brownstone steps to shoot each other with toy guns.

On rare occasion he was invited to the homes of well off classmates for their birthday parties on West End Avenue or Riverside Drive. In these beautiful and enormous pre-war spaces Marcus looked up in awe at the 20-foot ceilings, rich parquet floors and furnishings that made him feel inadequate and very out of place.

Marcus never forgot his origins and the fear of losing it all made him watchful and meticulous about his choices with money. He was generous but protected his investments like a keen accountant. The stories his mother shared about the pretty furniture and fancy rugs in these swanky homes she serviced was what got him interested in antiques and the business of acquisitions.

In the late 1980's after high school he found it necessary to disconnect from many childhood friends as they spiraled down into the Hell that was drug abuse. Too many friends were losing themselves to this world. He remained focused and traveled daily by subway down to Cooper Union where he obtained a degree in Arquitecture and Art History. His first love was Art history but knowing about structural design helped open numerous other doors.

By his late twenties he came to Infinity as director of Estate Acquisitions. This was an enviable position with perks galore, traveling to interesting places and mingling amongst the wealthy and powerful. Marcus was ready for a lifetime commitment to increase his capital and polish his image. To this day he had kept to his purpose and became a respected member of the industry.

La Mirabelle seemed out of place on a busy intersection right off of Central Park West. The lace curtained window looked more appropriate in a small town in France or even Paris than in the big concrete city that is New York. Once inside, they were welcomed warmly and escorted to their seats by the hostess and given a wine list. Marcus immediately ordered a chilled bottle of Krug Grand Cuvee champagne known for its crisp and delicious bouquet. As he looked deeply into Valentina's eyes he knew he had to lay the cards on the table and take this leap of faith. A pestering feeling of insecurity kept creeping up warning him that he could be jumping in too fast. Marcus decided that annoying feeling or not he was no longer pretending this was just a casual dinner amongst friends and colleagues.

He raised his champagne glass to make a toast, "Here's to you Valentina." Valentina smiled as he continued, "I have to tell you something that I have held in me for far too long." Marcus nervously cleared his throat and pushed on choosing his words carefully and despite his best intentions he said nervously, "I have strong feelings for you."

Valentina's smile dissipated. His words confused yet excited her at once. Not knowing how to react she kept a poker face as his piercing blue eyes searched her shiny brown ones. Feeling grateful when the waitress came, Valentina took a moment to think about what Marcus had shared. She wondered if she heard it correctly. Her eyes remained fixed on the menu as she read the same entrée over and over again. When the waitress asked her a third time if she was ready to order, Marcus put his warm large hand over her wrist. She looked up to his concerned eyes.

In a fluttery voice she excused her trance like appearance, "The champagne must have gone to my head. Sorry, I'll have the fish."

She closed the menu and looked at Marcus. He added two orders of grilled Portobello mushrooms on a bed of greens with goat cheese as appetizers, filet of sole for Valentina and a steak au poivre for himself. The waitress refreshed the champagne flutes and walked away with their order. Valentina took another sip of her drink before she looked up to meet Marcus. Although she felt flustered she knew this man was serious. His elbow rested on the table and his fist was balled up on his chin but his eyes were right on her. She wondered how difficult it was for him to open up his heart and how long he had wanted to declare his intentions.

He wants a response from me. I am so confused because I do like Marcus but I'm not over David yet, the tiny voice in her whispered.

She spoke carefully, "Marcus, I'm very flattered but I'm sort of reeling from this recent breakup just three weeks ago and now this announcement in the paper. I feel like I'm a big joke in New York. I'm so embarrassed and just need to be alone for awhile."

He did not show his deflated spirit but his heart was aching because what she didn't say was anything about him. He added, "Well, then just know that I am here always with you on my mind."

He looked at her intensely and waited for her response. Valentina swallowed hard and took another sip of champagne before she asked, "We have always gotten along but I never knew you had these feelings for me. Why now Marcus?"

Sighing deeply he looked away. Marcus decided not to hold back any longer and opened his heart.

"Valentina, all this time my love for you has grown from a spark of interest into knowing that my life without you has little meaning. But I will not pursue a one sided desire and have to know if I stand a chance," he took her hand and gently rubbed her knuckles with his thumb.

She watched his hands and noticed how strong they were. Around Marcus she had always felt safe and special. The tears welled in her eyes from feelings she did not fully understand but she did realize that Marcus was a very interesting man and one to be reckoned with. He took out his handkerchief and discreetly handed it to her. Valentina took a second to acknowledge how none of her other boyfriends ever had a handkerchief. She thought how chivalrous and old school Marcus was to carry one around. Dabbing the corners of her eyes she said barely above a whisper, "I never knew your feelings for me ran so deep." Her voice broke off and she looked down at her hands and continued quietly, "Marcus, give me time. I need to clear my head and yes I am attracted to you but I need time to clear out this past relationship. You understand, don't you?

Marcus straightened up and spoke calmly, "Yes I do. You already have my heart, take the time you need, and I will be here, no pressure but do not play games with me." She saw the sadness hiding behind his firm expression and gave him a half-hearted smile and was very thankful when their food came over.

The conversation over dinner was related to history, dogs, and travel and they found they laughed easily with one another on matters unrelated to work. By the time dinner ended, it had turned bitterly cold and they quickly returned to Valentina's apartment. After opening her apartment door she asked Marcus in, "Would you like to come in for a tea or coffee?" Marcus instead stared into her eyes and pulled her into his arms and kissed her on the mouth. His kiss was gentle at first but when she responded he unleashed his passion. He raked his fingers up through her hair until he was holding her head with one hand and her body close to his with the other. She had had good kissers before but Marcus was incomparable. When they separated, just barely leaving their lips he whispered, "Take my kiss with you and come back to me Valentina, my love for you is real." With these last words he kissed her again and released her, turned and walked to the elevators down the hall and around the corner.

Valentina was not dazed from champagne but from his kiss. She had never felt such ardor with other men while in their embrace. Locking the door and ignoring the bouncing dog at her feet she went straight to the bathroom. Staring back at herself she saw how flushed her cheeks and reddened her lips were. She could taste his fresh breath still in her mouth. It was very clear she felt strongly for him as well and the impulsive girl in her wanted to run out to tell him. But she resisted because somewhere very deep down Valentina understood that with Marcus there would be no need to rush or be impulsive.

Marcus entered his house feeling triumphant. He walked over to his Bose system and played Dizzy Gillespie's, A *Night in Tunisia*. Throughout the rest of the evening he slowly sipped on Johnny Walker Blue Label scotch and just let his mind wander over Valentina's lips, eyes and how good her body felt in his arms.

PART TWO

CHAPTER 7

Spain

It was 7 a.m. when the Virgin airlines flight landed safely in Barajas International Airport. Rain was coming down in pools of cold water and Valentina was anxious that Lola was not awakening from the Benadryl induced sleep. There was a car waiting with a short overweight driver whose jacket threatened to pop open from his enormous belly. He had a jovial personality and quickly loaded her luggage as she gently pulled the sleeping dog from the carryall. Throughout the downpour she tried to get Lola to awaken but to no avail. Finally reaching the hotel, she wrapped her up in her coat, grabbed her handbag and ran inside leaving the porter and driver to deal with the bags. She quickly checked in and was escorted to the suite overlooking the lush but very wet Parque del Retiro, Madrids lush and famous park. Laying Lola gently on the bed, the young dog continued to sleep soundly. Valentina looked around the room and caught sight of the arrangement of trilliums, roses and lilies with a lavender envelope to the side of the glass vase. Inhaling the flowers she relived the embrace and kiss she shared with Marcus.

As she read the note her smile widened, *"Each bloom carries my kiss; I wait for you, all my love, Marcus"*.

"Wow," Was the word that escaped from Valentina's lips. She welcomed this attention because her previous relationships were so flippant and by Marcus standards, immature. She undressed, showered and organized her clothing in the dressers and closets. Because it was raining, she ordered breakfast in her room and relaxed while rubbing Lola on her back. The pup slowly started to move about very groggily and stretched her hind legs. When she got her bearings and woke up she shook herself off and yawned loudly. Valentina grabbed her in a hug and filled her pretty face with kisses while expressing love and concern. Setting her down the pup immediately found the wee wee pad Valentina had set up in the bathroom and relieved herself after seven hours of traveling across the Atlantic.

When Valentina's breakfast arrived it was met by a barking dog and a nervous porter. Valentina spoke to him in Spanish to not be afraid of her dog and tipped him generously. Lola had her food and water while Valentina devoured the Spanish omelet, two cups of coffee, bread with marmalade and oatmeal cookies. The rain and wind were relentless throughout the day and into the next. They lounged around in the generous and fashionable suite and watched television, listened to music and ate. Valentina caught herself thinking about Marcus and that kiss that left her lips tingling and her body feeling warm and aroused.

It was six in the afternoon when the rain stopped in the wet and cold city. Valentina and Lola stepped out for a short run in the park to stretch their legs and returned drenched in sweat, dirty from wet grass and mud and chilled to the bone. After a warm bath and a light dinner Valentina picked up her phone to check the messages. There were voicemails from the Spain auction house that she decided to answer shortly and a few texts from colleagues about acquisitions and sales information but nothing from Marcus. She took the initiative and dialed his cell phone. In New York it was just about noon when most meetings were over and Marcus would probably be behind his desk. The phone rang three times before Marcus' voice responded with a sexy laugh, "I thought you'd never call."

Hearing his laugh was reassuring to her. "When we arrived the rain was intense and I was exhausted. It just stopped about two hours ago."

"I miss you," said Marcus softly

"Me too," whispered Valentina feeling absurd at saying these very words to her boss.

"A month is impossibly long Valentina," his voice carried a slight desperation.

"It is a long time but I did ask for a little time, remember. I need to clear my head," said Valentina gently.

His sigh of resignation sounded heavily over the line. There was an awkward silence until Valentina added, "Marcus, the flowers are beautiful, thank you for being so thoughtful."

"I'm sorry for being pushy, I just want you in my life and now we are an ocean apart. I should not say this. I have no real idea how you feel yet and here I am blubbering about my feelings. I guess it's just that it has been a long time for me and after our kiss the other night I have done nothing but think about you," Marcus said tiredly.

"Thank you Marcus for flattering me. I needed to hear something special like that." There was nothing else she could say because she wanted to be certain of her own feelings. Instead of feeding into more of his discontent Valentina changed the subject. "I see the estate in an hour and will start with salon pieces." She tried to sound excited.

Valentina's job was exciting and the perks were generous but at this moment she wanted nothing more than to be back in New York in Marcus' arms receiving one of those passionate kisses that left her desiring more. Marcus asked with concern after a long pause in their conversation, "Valentina, are you there, hello?"

Valentina awoke from her daydreams to respond, "Of course I'm here Marcus. Sorry, I was thinking of this apartment." She lied to not seem foolish. "I better get going to be there in time. I expect Sotheby's will be like hungry wolves snatching up everything with any value."

"Yes, do that and let me know what you think will work for Infinity. I understand these are mostly Deco pieces which always sell very well here," Marcus added.

"I will call you later tonight your time around eleven which would be about five in the morning here if that is alright with you?"

"That's at the crack of dawn. Isn't five in the morning to early for you?" Marcus asked curiously.

"Actually, it's my usual wake up time in New York. This way I can run with Lola and get ready," Valentina explained.

"Okay, call me anytime and I mean that. Be safe."

"Thank you again for the flowers. So long." Her heart raced a bit from the conversation and because she did not really want it to end. Valentina did not remember when a man had made her feel so safe and loved except for her father. This caused her to remember him. To Valentina her father was larger than life, boisterous, happy and always swooping her up into the air. Her eyes grew misty when she recalled how he would fill her face and dimples with kisses. Before the tears threatened to surface, she busied herself with getting ready for the visit.

CHAPTER 8

El Portón

The tiny Fiat cab whisked Valentina across the park to the other side of the Retiro neighborhood. Retiro is a large family oriented neighborhood with cafes and boutiques. The famous park defines the entire neighborhood with its elegant fountains and statues. El Parque Del Buen Retiro or as Madrileños call it, El Retiro, boasts some of the most tranquil and beautifully designed green spaces in all of Spain. Valentina's hotel was by Puerta Alcala and the apartment building she was visiting was about half a mile across the park. When her cab approached the building, Valentina prepared the payment and asked him to stop on the corner. At a café, she purchased a café con leche and took it to go. Walking up the street gave Valentina a chance to people watch. There were young families and many smartly dressed people hurrying along.

El Portón was the name of the building and judging from its large, heavy, black metal doors one could understand why it was called this way. The doors were bronze, very ornate with large rounded handles. Pressing a disc to the right opened the enormous doors that led to a well-tended courtyard. Valentina looked around and saw graceful trees fronting the entrance to the elegant building. A graceful fountain of nymphs pouring water into a pond graced the center of the courtyard. The fountain had just enough patina to give it an antiqued and aged appearance. Between each tree there were black iron benches large enough for two with polished wood seats. From where Valentina stood facing the fountain she had a direct view to the doors that entered the building. The beauty of the courtyard mesmerized her and despite the cold, she wanted to linger a while but she had work to do.

Glass and wrought iron filigreed doors opened with ease onto a handsome marble floored foyer with a graceful staircase to the right and a large arrangement of a variety of flowers expertly displayed upon a rounded pedestal wood table. The first two floors of El Porton was a marbled walkup with handsomely carved mahogany banisters and more wrought iron filigree work. The remaining five flights up led to the apartments that flanked either side of the building and could only be reached by elevator or a side stairwell that was not as impressive as the main staircase.

After walking up two flights, Valentina stopped on the second floor and counted only two apartments one on either side. This meant these spaces were each no less than 2,000 square feet. Guessing at the size of these spaces excited her because it meant one of two things; either the place she was going to visit was packed with period pieces or filled with worthless junk. Instinctively, she knew that only an affluent person could live at this desired address and probably would not have furniture from a big box store. The stairs were directly in front of a small glass enclosed elevator that lifted guests and tenants to the remaining five flights. Upon entering she admired the beautifully carved wood that surrounded rectangular pieces of thick mottled glass. The elevator ran smoothly up to the seventh floor and stopped quietly. Unlike the other floors the entire seventh floor was one penthouse. A singular apartment with two large, heavy, wood doors faced the elevators. The floors outside of the apartment were different with a smart interchanging white and black marble tile pattern. Valentina pressed the bell to the side of the massive double doors and waited. After she silently counted to twenty and wondered if she should leave, the sounds of someone unlocking the door from within were heard. The door to the right opened slowly to reveal a small thin woman wearing a dark taupe dress that looked like a uniform. She wore small gold-rimmed glasses on her tiny face and had her neat bob pulled back with a tortoise colored shell hair band. Her voice was as petite as she, "Buenas tardes, es usted la señorita Valentina Puig? Valentina smiled and extended her hand but the woman just looked at her and grinned.

"Hola, soy Valentina Puig y represento el almacen Infinity Acquisitions de New York."

"Si, si, pase por favor." The woman opened the door ushering Valentina into a large empty foyer. She stepped upon Italian pink marble and noticed the foyer had a large wall where a grand painting at one point hung. Valentina knew this because the paint in the large rectangular space was several shades darker from the remainder of the faded wall. Two tall, ornate and polished wood doors flanked either side of the twenty-foot wall. Intricately carved moldings decorated the perimeter of the ceilings giving one the sense of being in a large wedding cake. Valentina looked down and noticed the matching decorated moldings along the baseboard and pink marbled floor.

The woman introduced herself, "Mi nombre es Costanza Linares de Palacios. Pase por aquí, si es tan amable." Valentina followed the woman through the right door noticing immediately that the left door flanking the foyer wall would have led to the same enormous sitting room. The room had very few pieces of furniture but they were rich luxury items. Valentina salivated at the thought of acquiring these pieces. She was pleased that the other two auction houses had not yet arrived to stake a claim thus giving her ample time to put in proposals for the coveted pieces. Everything about this room screamed Art Deco period, from the chiseled frosted glass sconces to the burl wood desks, tables, chairs and torchieres. The place was immaculate, airy and the scent of lemon verbena gently danced around adding to the elegance of the space.

Eager to get the story on the space, Valentina started asking questions in Spanish. "Señora, what happened to the lady who lived here?"

The petite woman sat off to the side on a chair not from the collection Valentina was viewing. She quietly shared her story, "If you don't mind my heavy accent I will speak in English to practice with you, okay?'

Valentina was surprised but quickly acknowledged with a wave and a smile that English was fine. Costanza offered her a seat on one of two of the coveted Edward Wormley Y back captains chairs by the fireplace. Valentina carefully took a seat and secretly enjoyed the supple sienna colored leather and soft elegant wood on the arm rests. Costanza continued, "La Duquesa Isabella del Conde lived here for over 80 years. She purchased this apartment when she was in her twenties. When she moved in, my mother was her lady, perhaps you would call it servant but we are caretakers of the family and home. That is much more than just a servant. There were servants, many, many servants and chefs but only the women in my family looked after La Duquesa."

Valentina noticed the pride this woman spoke with. She admired people who took their work seriously. Valentina continued to listen attentively.

"Three months ago at the age of 104 she passed away in her sleep like a little bird in a nest." The woman looked away and glanced at the window draped in dupione silk toile curtains with a pastoral design of shepherds, hills and farm animals. Valentina sat quietly giving the woman who appeared to be in her sixties a chance to continue her story.

Looking forlornly Costanza continued, "She never married or had children but she had many lovers and she loved to have parties. She was in her nineties and still having parties, Díos mio! But she was like a mother to me and she wanted her beloved home to be well cared for. In her Will she left everything here to me. I was the child she never had and she doted on me."

Valentina could not believe this woman was now the owner. She wondered if Costanza understood anything about provenance and value. Certainly each piece would garner a hefty sum at auction if they ever got to that but would this woman be wise enough to understand the process. Not wasting any time Valentina probed, "Señora, are attorneys involved in the sale of these pieces? I mean obviously there are attorneys because we knew of this apartment through the announcement of the estate being sold. What I would like to know is if the auction houses that aren't here yet are aware that you are the current owner and not the Duquesa del Conde?"

The woman looked somewhat puzzled yet confidently responded, "Perhaps I look simple to you but I am not ignorant to the value of these pieces. I was taught by La Duquesa herself and instructed on what to do and who to contact. It was the very Duquesa who told me about your company because her New York apartment was decorated by a famous designer from your store in the 1960's."

Blushing at her indiscretion Valentina responded apologetically, "Oh, I never meant to imply you were naïve of such things, I do apologize if…"

"Tranquila, relax. You did not offend me. Americans think people who devote themselves to the service of royalty or rich families are simple-minded but we are often intelligent and well educated ourselves. I myself studied art appreciation for two semesters at Le Sorbonne in Paris while La Duquesa lived in that beautiful city but when we returned to Madrid I continued my studies here at Universidad Autonóma instead. Well, would you like some té or café?"

"Tea would be fine, thank you," Valentina smiled shyly.

Costanza turned slightly and pressed a buzzer. She turned around again to face Valentina and smiled.

"Why don't you look around before the others arrive, make yourself at home and feel free to wander into the other rooms?"

Costanza stood and gestured while explaining, "To my right is the dining room which seats twenty four, followed by the kitchen, two servants quarters that sleep four, the chefs bedroom, two bathrooms at the end and a sitting room for the service. To your left there are four bedrooms each with bathrooms and large closets. There is also a little sitting room where we kept a television and place for the men to smoke and play cards or chess during parties. These French doors lead out to a wrap around balcony. There you will find outdoor furniture and many beautiful planters from around the world. La Duquesa collected them particularly from Morocco and Italy."

Valentina quickly took out her iPad mini and started to take photos of all the pieces. She walked around the bedrooms and marveled at the beautiful mahogany wood sleigh beds and mirrored vanities with gently bent wood in varying amber hues. There was a mid century Eames rocker casually poised by a pair of French doors, numerous Marcel Breuer chairs and loungers and Donald Deskey dressers in every room. It was like stepping back in time to the decades of the 30's through the 50's. It was obvious that the deceased duchess loved Deco and American minimalism. To Valentina's surprise and disappointment there were no decorative pieces or art hanging from the walls. Tell tale signs of faded paint on the walls kept secrets as to their whereabouts. She made a mental note to inquire with Costanza.

A short man in a waistcoat and tails surprised Valentina, as she was about to enter the master bedroom. He gestured towards the sitting room where an elaborate tea service was displayed. Costanza asked her, "Do sit and enjoy some tea and cakes. Have you seen any interesting pieces for your company Miss Puig?"Valentina sat while the man poured tea into stunning cream, black and gold-rimmed deco cups and saucers. She could not take her eyes off the simple yet graceful swirled lines of the flatware. Details such as these would be lost on most people butValentina had a discriminating eye for minutiae. She knew she had to have the dishes and flatware for herself. Taking the cup and saucer in her hand she tasted the gentle Oolong tea and smiled at Costanza, "I love it all Señora. Actually, this happens to be my favorite style in interior design. I cannot help but admire this setting and the flatware is gorgeous."

Valentina knew she sounded like she hit a Wednesday shoe sale at Macy's with coupons and she did not care. It was rare when she had the opportunity to work with this design style. Too often, estates were filled with heavy, traditional and predictable ornate pieces. They are beautiful and important in their own right. Contrarily, Art Deco was very sexy, clean and modern at a time when modernism was not appreciated. Deco was and remains decidedly very American.

The doorbell chimed and two men and a tall, glamorous blond were ushered into the sitting room.Valentina felt herself grow sick to her stomach when she recognized the woman.

Oh my God, what is she doing here? What could she possibly want with all this? This is the woman David left me for. Valentina thought. She relaxed her features to not give away her anxiety and sipped more tea. She felt like her insides were being squeezed. Feeling faint from the shallow breathing and shock she breathed deeply to collect herself before anyone noticed.

The two men, Ramón Gutierrez andAnthony Ruiz both represented Sotheby's and the blond was the heiress Diana Monroe, their client.

Costanza shared an abridged version of the story behind the apartment leaving out her current ownership. Valentina suspected she did not want to deal with these people from her colder manner towards them. Costanza stood taller, looked haughtier and had an air of entitlement that Valentina had not seen earlier. Something was definitely amiss.

The blond was expensively dressed in an oyster gray Celine wrap dress and Manolo Blahnik sling back gray, crocodile heels. She carried a pink crocodile Berkin bag off her left forearm and an off white Armani alpaca coat draped casually on her shoulders. The outfit was an easy $150,000 and Valentina took it all in through a phony smile that hid her increasing anxiety. Introductions were made and Diana Monroe looked back curiously at Valentina. She stopped walking and asked her directly, "You look familiar. Whom do you represent?"

Valentina remained calm and responded, "I represent Infinity Acquisitions in New York City."

Monroe gave a little laugh and dismissively said, "Oh, I'm on the board of directors for the company. Then you must work with Marcus Napier."

So she knows Marcus and is on the board too, crap. Valentina thought to herself.

Diana Monroe looked Valentina up and down and turned to follow the men she came in with. Valentina glared at the woman as she walked away.

The men went about writing and photographing all the pieces while explaining to Diana Monroe the possible worth in their heavily accented English.

Not missing a beat, Costanza noticed the change in Valentina's complexion when she saw Diana Monroe. The astute woman made a mental note to herself about this and proceeded with the clients. Following them from room to room and leaving Valentina in the sitting room she listened carefully as Diana Monroe dismissed room after room of the furnishings with a wave of her manicured hands. Costanza remained silent as she observed the demanding woman and the men who acted like dogs groveling to please their master.

It was turning dark and colder and her head was hurting along with her back. Valentina knew when she was stressed because her head and back were the recipients of all her anxieties. Some people eat, others drink but Valentina just hurts.

She wanted to leave but if she did then she would not be able to stake claim to the pieces her company would benefit from the most. She decided to see the master bedroom and started to walk over when she noticed that everyone was already there. Diana Monroe was soft spoken but firm, "I want all of these pieces and the apartment. Establish provenance and value and send it to my attorneys, they will handle the rest."

Valentina nearly fainted when she saw the room. All the furniture items were authentically mirrored Art Deco period pieces that were difficult to find. The vanity was low with dark, rounded burl wood sides. Two pieces of floating glass were held in place by a moon made of alabaster rising above the surface. The large rounded mirror graced the vanity and was held by two bold ebony statues of nude muscled men. The bed was a four-poster King with mirrors inlaid in creamy, chocolate wood. The headboard was all beveled mirrored squares held together by gilded pieces of wood. There was a Wormley console with the gentle half wave design in a darker wood and on the floor the rug was a Kandinsky masterpiece.

Costanza read the distress in Valentina's eyes. She quickly spoke up with authority stunning both men and Diana Monroe, "This room has already been spoken for by Miss Puig and the apartment is not for sale."

Diana Monroe was not a woman who took the word "no" easily. In fact, she never really heard the word from anyone because her life had been one of extreme privilege and entitlement. She looked at the diminutive woman from above with a certain degree of distaste.

Costanza stood as tall as she could and spoke clearly though with a heavier accent, "I am afraid you do not understand, I own this apartment and everything in it. It is I who will not sell the apartment because this is my home. As for the contents of this room, provenance and value was already established by Miss Puig from Infinity Acquisitions. Now your time here has ended and I politely ask that you take your leave. Mr. Ruiz and Mr. Gutierrez you will contact me tomorrow and we will make a final appointment. Goodbye Ms. Monroe."

Costanza gave a tight smile to all and turned on her heel. Diana Monroe's look could wilt flowers. She turned to the Sotheby representatives and spit venom, "You assured me I would have first take at this and I come all this way to waste my time!" The woman stormed away leaving two desperately nervous and irate men with their mouths opened. Monroe turned back and walked up to Valentina and said in a cool tone, "Good job obtaining these for Infinity but I'll talk to Marcus as he always pleases me. He and I go way back and he owes me a favor."

The men followed calling out her name but when Gutierrez spotted Valentina he came up to her and called her a derogatory term, "Zorra!" The term fox when used in this tone in Spanish meant nothing beautiful but rather made reference to cunning, calculating women of questionable reputations. The word stung Valentina and it froze her in place. It happens to everyone from time to time when someone hits so below the belt with a surprise comment that it leaves you temporarily in shock and without a comeback line.

Costanza hearing it all spoke up firmly, "Gutierrez, in my house no lady is ever disrespected. Don't bother calling me tomorrow y fuera de aquí." The butler handed out coats to the embarrassed men. Diana Monroe was already on the elevator heading down and agitatedly talking on her cell phone.

Costanza turned around and saw the tears blurring Valentina's eyes. She took her by the forearm and escorted her to the sitting room. There, Valentina tried in vain to suppress her tears but she could not hold them back. She looked away but Costanza took her chin and said gently, "Hablame, who is that woman with her nose so close to the sky she could touch the clouds. That woman, I do not like at all."

Glancing at her watch Valentina saw that it was already nine in the evening and Lola had to be walked and fed. She rummaged for her cell phone in her bag and called the hotel concierge. The concierge assured her that a busboy would immediately walk Lola and feed her. She needed to get distracted to compose herself enough to give Costanza some semblance of logic.

Taking a deep breath she shared with Costanza her recent break up and the announcement in The New York Times. Costanza listened calmly and bobbed her head from time to time. She liked Valentina and she wasn't sure why but there was something about her honest eyes and casual style that made her feel comfortable around her. When Valentina finished she took some water that had been poured for her throughout her recounting. Both women took deep breaths. The pain of betrayal is something so deep and hurtful that it can tear at the core of a person's confidence and this is what was happening to Valentina. She had before her very eyes the woman David had chosen over her. It wasn't a beauty contest because both women were stunning but it was a question of why and her suspicions were confirmed today. Diana Monroe was wealthy, beautiful and accomplished. Valentina Puig came from humble beginnings, is beautiful and accomplished. But David always wanted prestige and with Diana Monroe as his wife he could enter a world where only a select few people on the planet would ever come to know. Valentina realized that while she shopped at Bergdorf Goodman's, Diana Monroe could easily own the store. Here was where their differences existed and similarities ended.

Valentina sighed deeply and knew this wasn't because she was lacking but because David was a man of little confidence and self-respect. He was a respected doctor but a physician attached to Diana Monroe's prestige and name would travel in distinct circles of the wealthy and famous and never need to practice medicine himself. Money like that could buy him hospital wings with his name in large brass letters while he sunbathed on a yacht in the Mediterranean.

Valentina thanked Costanza for her kindness and asked her, "I understand you did not like Ms. Monroe but how did you know I would love every piece in the master bedroom?"

Costanza took Valentina's hand and squeezed it, "Because querida, this is my favorite period too and I saw your eyes come alive when you stepped into La Duquesa's room."

They hugged and Valentina walked with Costanza to the foyer where the diminutive man waited with her coat in his forearm. As she was helped with her coat she shared with Costanza, "There's quite a bit here for me to do. I already have provenance but I have to establish value and those men from Sotheby's won't be of any help. I will call my boss later but when can I return?"

Costanza laughed, "Come back tomorrow around noon and bring Lola. I want to meet this little dog and you can have lunch here. We will make a nice caldo and something to eat like some delicious pan con tomate. ¿Está bien?" Valentina thanked Costanza and they hugged again. The butler looked up at Valentina and very gallantly said, "Buenas Noches señorita." Valentina gave the kind faced man a broad genuine smile that obviously fed his ego and responded, "Graciás a usted y buenas noches."

They waited at the door until she entered the elevator and waved as she headed down. Valentina waved back. When she reached the courtyard she stepped out to a cold night with a clear starry sky. The trees that lined the foyer were illuminated with fairy lights that gave the place a magical, ethereal quality. She sat on a cold bench to breathe in the crisp air and wondered exactly what favor Marcus owed this woman. Valentina surprised herself at how uncomfortable she was with Diana Monroe's quip about Marcus pleasing her or owing her a favor. Turning her attention to the fountain, she closed her eyes and inhaled another breath of cold air. It was so pretty to stand amidst the lights in the courtyard that Valentina took smaller steps to make the journey to the front gate last longer.

Once outside the large doors of El Portón, she hailed a cab and headed back to the hotel. Madrid was abuzz with people heading back and forth. Work ended around seven in the evening and restaurants did not serve dinner until after nine. Valentina only had the breakfast in her stomach and the tea at Costanza's home. She needed a shower, dinner and to be with her fuzzy, four legged baby. Somehow, after sharing her sorrows with Costanza, Valentina did not feel so alone, she actually could breathe deeply and felt fine. The sting of betrayal was still there and she understood this would take time to heal but she was hopeful and in thinking this it was Marcus that came to mind. But Diana Monroe clouded his face and left Valentina with an uneasy feeling.

CHAPTER 9

Old Memories

After a hot shower, Valentina's stressed muscles relaxed enough to induce an appetite. With a light dinner of potato soup and crusty bread with red wine she felt mellow and calm. She continued to de-stress by watching a little television before she called Marcus. She and Lola curled up in bed to watch the 1948 British film, *The Red Shoes*. It was a dubbed version and exactly what Valentina needed to relax. Ballet was one of her favorite indulgences and this movie hit the spot. It was romantic and tragic much like she felt her own life to be. Both dozed off to sleep to the haunting musical score by Brian Easdale under the cozy warmth of the down comforter. It was almost five the next morning when she awoke to get some water and remembered to call Marcus. Searching for her cell in her bag she dialed his number and walked out of the bedroom to the living room where she settled into an over tufted cream chaise lounge. She was sleepy but she had too much to share with Marcus. The phone rang several times before he picked up.

"Wow, It's exactly 5 a.m. in Spain, did you have the front desk call you?" asked Marcus.

Valentina was processing his question, "What? No, that's just my internal clock."

"Well, that is some precision clock inside of you. Tell me, how did your visit go?"

"It was not an easy day yesterday. You won't believe everything that happened. How much time do you have?" she added quietly.

"For you, I have all the time in the world, tell me everything Valentina, just let me hear your voice."

I love to hear your voice too, thought Valentina

Speaking slowly and with exhaustion in her voice, Valentina shared the events of the day. She shared all the job related details; the special qualities of the apartment and El Porton, and of course her encounter with Diana Monroe. Marcus listened attentively uttering an occasional, *Uh huh and really.*

When she finished she suppressed a yawn and waited for his response. Marcus sensed the sleepiness and stress in her voice and offered, "If you want, you can come back home and we can send someone else to complete this job." He thought she might prefer to let someone complete the transactions.

Valentina quickly responded, "No way, this is perhaps the biggest acquisition I have ever obtained with solid provenance and incredible value. It's not a few pieces we are talking about but almost an entire apartment with nearly 4,000 square feet of genuine furniture. Oh my goodness, Marcus, the master bedroom is a dream. I wish I could own a vanity and bed like that."

Valentina came alive again and he could tell she was smiling as she talked about her favorite design style. Then he noticed her voice develop a cloudy quality that he interpreted as fear.

"Marcus, Monroe was livid that the owner would not sell the apartment and bedroom pieces directly to her. She stormed out saying she would talk to you and that you owed her a favor and something about you two going way back."

Marcus took a sip from his scotch whiskey and added, "Diana Monroe is nothing in my life. Don't give her a second thought. She's just annoyed because she did not get her way but it sounds to me like you have the current owner in your pocket."

"Costanza is a sweetheart. I know you will love her because she's such a genuine person. I was invited to have lunch with her and she invited Lola as well." He laughed and puffed on his cigar adding, "Today will be a better day my sweet and I doubt Sotheby will be back anytime soon."

Valentina had this feeling that Marcus might know Monroe intimately because she recalled hearing gossip some years ago that he was dating a very young socialite a year after his wife died. She hesitated but finally had to ask, "Marcus, how well do you know Monroe? You know what I mean, did you two ever date?" Marcus wished she had not asked but he would not lie to her. He cleared his throat before responding, "Yes, we dated some years ago."

The silence from Valentina was deafening. "Oh, I had no idea but figured you two would know each other through all the events and the company," Valentina tried to sound like this confirmation had not bothered her. "Valentina, it was a long time ago and short lived, please don't read anything into this." Marcus worried that with her sensitive emotional state she would not be able to see things clearly.

She got up and walked over to the large floor to ceiling windows and stared out at the lights that spread out across the old, historical city. Marcus guardedly started to say, "Vale…" when Valentina interrupted him, "Marcus, uh, no worries, it's like you said, it was a long time ago. I'm really tired. You have a good day okay, "she chirped though the discontent was coming through.

Knowing when to back away when all was lost was something Marcus knew how to do. He knew she needed time and space to process all this information. She was getting hit from every angle and now he had contributed too more hurt. Ending on a high note was important to him, "I want you to have a wonderful day. If you like we can talk later."

"Sure, have a good day," an abrupt and cold silence was what Marcus heard on the other end. He finished his scotch and angrily crushed the partially smoked expensive cigar into the waste bin. His night just started off on the wrong foot.

The rest of the morning had Valentina in a fitful sleep. She tossed and turned and could not rest. All she could think about was how this woman Diana Monroe was everywhere in her life. She wanted to be able to start over elsewhere and not ever face anyone in New York. Thinking too much gave her a headache that prompted her to jump into the shower and blast her body with cold water. Shivering and teeth chattering she threw on her running gear then twisted her long hair in a high ponytail and took Lola out for a run.

It was 6:30 in the morning and Madrid was just barely opening its big Spanish eyes. The sun shone brightly and though the weather was brisk it was deliciously perfect for a good run. The four-year old Jack Russell jogged alongside Valentina as they entered the quiet park.

El Retiro started out as several acres of recreation for the Royal court around the year 1630. It was land bequeathed to King Philip IV by Count-Duke de Olivares Gaspar de Guzman. Throughout the years as different heads of state ruled, the park went through several metamorphoses from open land to a green space with gardens, museums, statues, and ponds.

Together they ran past numerous statues of former Kings and Queens of Spain, several ponds and the beautiful statue of The Fallen Angel. She stopped here to admire the statue and catch her breath. Lola was panting and looking excitedly up at her master. Bending down to stroke Lola's back, she looked at her sports watch and saw that they had been running a half hour. Another half hour back and this would be a great run and tire out Lola enough to give her an hour or so of naptime. They wrapped around the fountain and ran back through a more shaded area with magnificent trees and walkways.

Retiro certainly did justice to its name that translated meant to rest, to repose. It was pleasing to Valentina that during the hour they ran she only saw three sanitation workers raking leaves and an elderly man throwing chunks of bread into a pond to feed a family of ducks.

Upon reaching the hotel and entering the lobby, Valentina hurried up to her room not wanting to be noticed too much in her workout gear and perspiring face. Not many Europeans followed the exercise craze of Americans. They favored exercise such as walking and Yoga to running and overly exerting themselves. Many European cities were pedestrian friendly and to see and feel the city it was best to walk everywhere. Men and women in Madrid as in Paris and London were stylish, fit and very chic. It was unheard of to leave your home undone. Going market shopping required some fashion sense and a comb through the hair with a little gloss on the lips. Women always took their appearances seriously. It was easy work to spot the European from the American tourist. No one was ever seen wearing sloppy sweats or trainers or God forbid shorts around the streets. Sports shoes were for the gym or exercise and never for any other activity.

After a calming bath for herself and a separate one for Lola they tucked into their respective breakfast and napped for an hour. Awakening refreshed she stood before the floor length windows overlooking the park. Thinking how this suite could have used a terrace reminded Valentina of how she never got to see the one at El Portón. Valentina dressed, drank the remaining orange juice and finished another half of toast with blueberry jam. She threw on her jeans and boots, a fitted sweater, scarf and coat. Keeping the jewelry to just earrings and a set of gold bangles, Valentina proceeded to El Portón with a walk across the park.

With all of nature around her, she took this time to reflect and in doing so she realized how stressed she had felt always trying to keep up with the social circles David desperately wanted to be a member of. She recalled a bitter argument they had over his not wanting to travel up to the Bronx because it was an outer borough. Tía Carmela was too far and in the wrong place for David to visit. She recalled an angry exchange when she asked, "If she lived in Scarsdale would you go?" David shouted, "Yes!" and slammed her apartment door as he exited.

For the past three weeks Valentina had been numb from the breakup, then sick over the engagement and just now she was starting to see the light at the end of the tunnel. But although elitist, conceited and a general ass, it was two years of her life she spent traveling, eating, socializing, kissing and sleeping with David. Three weeks was a short time to get anyone out of your head or move on with someone else.

They were almost on the other side of the park as Valentina caught herself smiling at the hopefulness of a fresh start. She thought of Marcus and how he was growing on her. It surprised her how she looked forward to hearing his voice even though Diana Monroe was like an albatross hanging over their possible budding romance.

Later today, she decided, she would call to share the work and chat. This time she wanted love to grow and go slowly. Her time with David was too often one of bitter arguments that led to his slamming doors, storming out, and then calling apologetically in an obvious stoned or drunken state. Valentina tried in vain to keep things together in their relationship because she loved him. Just as she was nearing the other side of the park she recalled another argument that had sent shivers down her spine. David had picked her up at work in his BMW and was obviously stoned. She had pleaded with him to slow down on the northbound FDR Drive but all she got in return was he shouting her down. When they arrived at her apartment he collapsed on her bed and fell asleep while she just sat in the living room shaken to the bone. Despite her better judgment she went through his pockets and she found four tiny orange pills. After investigating online with the site, pillfinder.com, it confirmed that David was taking oxycontin.

The next morning after a sleepless night she confronted a very groggy David as he exited the shower. After a huge blowout where David did what he could to spin his story around and act offended that his pockets had been violated Valentina knew the end was near. Again he stormed out shouting expletives and slamming the front door causing Mrs. Hilfstein from apartment 6D to open her door to see where all the noise was coming from.

Valentina recalled the coldness in the pit of her stomach on that day. As she reached the edge of the park she wondered what kept her in a sick relationship instead of moving on. Being introspective about her life, Valentina thought, *what does it say about me to have remained with David for as long as I did? I was such a jerk wasting my time with him.*

Why had she tolerated such bad behavior and put up with an obvious drug problem? This and other questions were what she pondered over again and again.

Throughout their final months together David was careful never to let Valentina catch him with any pills or drug paraphernalia. He took measures to only see her when he was clean and sober. But Valentina noticed other behaviors that confirmed there was indeed a problem such as his constant scratching, limited to no appetite and sometimes slurred speech. Staying when the ship was sinking is what kept her up too many nights and she wondered if she would still be on this doomed vessel had he not broken up with her.

CHAPTER 10

Days of Wine and Roses

Costanza and her staff could not be more accommodating with Valentina and Lola. A large bed pillow had been placed under the window in the sitting room for Lola to rest upon. There were treats and a toy for her to play with as well. The little dog played with the staff while Valentina carefully and meticulously wrote detailed descriptions of the items in two rooms.

She had to determine types of woods, patina, paint, metals, stone, and numerous other details. It was a time consuming task and by six p.m. she had only done the two smaller bedrooms, which were each about 400 square feet, the size of a typical New York City apartment. The apartment was enormous with plenty of furniture to review. Valentina was left alone to work while Lola entertained everyone. From the bedrooms, she heard the service people say in Spanish, "Preciosa perrita," "Qué guapa," "Parece una niña de tan juguetona." She smiled at the comments on how pretty and playful her pup was and how much fun she brought to this house. Two of the men were on their knees throwing a little ball and enjoying watching Lola catch and release as the women clapped away.

Valentina entered to this scene and when Lola saw her she ran over and jumped up to be carried. After placing the iPad down she carried Lola, planted a kiss on her cheek which Lola returned by licking the tip of Valentina's nose causing everyone to make collective sounds of, *Ah* and *Aw*.

The service returned to their respective tasks and Valentina took this opportunity before leaving to ask Costanza about the outdoor space. "Would it be alright if I saw the terrace?"

Costanza quickly rose from her chair and opened the large French doors with a key. She ushered Valentina outside to an enormous, spacious terrace. The terrace was a wrap around extending 20 feet in width and 1,200 feet in length. It had beautiful mosaic planters that were currently empty due to the weather and some wrapped fruit trees to protect them from the cold. There were many matching teak wood chairs covered and off to the side along with sun loungers, a large rectangular table, retrievable sunshades, and a very old covered hot tub off outside of the master bedroom. Valentina's eyebrows went up as she imagined all the sexual debauchery that took place in that hot tub over the decades.

The sheer size of the space had Valentina amazed with the possibilities for decorating. It was common for her to pretend to live in some of the magnificent homes she visited but this apartment had replaced them all with its old world charm and character.

When she re-entered the apartment she found Costanza sitting down with her hands folded on her lap and Lola resting at her feet. "I see Lola likes you Costanza," said Valentina with a smile.

Costanza moved her hand down the spine of the dog making Lola's tail wiggle excitedly. "She knows I am a good person and I love animals. Dogs can sense who is kind and who is not. Tell me, what did you think of all you did today?"

"Wow, I'm overwhelmed to be honest. This apartment is a dream and that terrace is just waiting for a fantastic party," Valentina added.

"I told you how La Duquesa was always having parties here and she often entertained her gentlemen friends in the hot tub, she was wild in her younger years, may she rest in peace," Costanza said making the sign of the cross.

"My goodness! So how old is that hot tub?" Valentina furrowed her eyebrows questioningly.

Costanza laughed and touched her chest as she explained; "La Duquesa was very active with her lovers well into her seventies. That hot tub has seen many parties, let me see, I think it's at least 40 years old because I was in my twenties when she had it installed and by then she was already in her 60's. Her life was rich in all aspects."

Valentina had not realized her large almond shaped eyes were wide open causing Costanza to laugh even harder and continue, "For all her wild ways let me tell you she was beloved of all of us. All her servants' children went to excellent schools and universities or learned a trade thanks to her. That's why we are so devoted to her things and memory. We absolutely loved her."

Valentina added, "What a generous woman. I see why you are so particular of what she has left to you. Did you have your own family, Costanza?" The woman looked down and shook her head sadly to respond, "The man I loved was an American colonel but he died just before the Vietnam War ended. We wanted to marry and have a family but he felt a duty to his country. I just never met anyone else and stayed here as La Duquesa's personal assistant."

"I'm sorry. It must have been so difficult for you," said Valentina.

"When a great love is lost it is almost impossible to recover in another. It has been lonely and more so since La Duquesa died because we were very close and loved each other like mother and daughter. Valentina, when true, honest love comes to you, because let me tell you, that David was not it, you will know. Safeguard it and fight for it." Costanza sighed and smiled sadly at Valentina.

They sat quietly until Costanza broke the silence with her question, "So my dear when are you returning? Valentina smiled at her and said, "You know I need a few more days because there is so much and I can't wait to evaluate the master bedroom. I will contact my assistant Cecilia to come and help me with this task. Would it be alright if I return Monday morning around ten or eleven?"

Costanza walked over to a beautiful art deco half moon table. She opened the drawer and took out a set of keys arranged on a ring with a blue silk tassle. Walking over to Valentina, Costanza counted the keys and handed them over to her saying, "This coming week, I will be in Barcelona visiting my mother who is in her eighties. I gave the rest of the service the week to relax and go home so why don't you let yourself in and lock up when you leave." Valentina could not believe the trust this woman had in her. She had never been given keys before and felt quite special. She immediately expressed her gratitude, "Thank you so much. In this way I can come in early and be finished by next Friday. Thank you for your faith in me."

"I know you have a good heart. Enjoy the space, help yourself to anything in the kitchen and I will see you in one week," Costanza went to get up when Valentina remembered to ask, "I just have to know, what happened to all the art that I was expecting to find such as the sculptures, paintings, etcetera?" Costanza gave a smirk while explaining; "You remember those two characters from Sotheby's? Well they came not two days after La Duquesa died and we were all in Sevilla at her wake and burial. They obtained keys from her lawyer because the auction house was named in the will and came in here and took all the paintings and sculptures and prepared them for auction. So when I came back I immediately called my attorneys, filed a suit against the lawyer and Sotheby's. For now the art is in court ordered storage until matters are resolved. No one can touch it."

Valentina could not believe the brazenness of those two men. As she got up to leave she gathered Lola's leash and picked up after the tired dog despite Costanzas pleas to leave the mess alone. But Valentina fluffed the pillows and picked up toys and papers that were strewn about by Lola. The sitting room was once again as it was when they arrived. She added as she put her coat on, "I cannot believe those two men."

Costanza huffed her remarked, "They are not men, they are vultures. But they will regret this if they haven't already."

"Well, thank you once again for everything and enjoy visiting with your mother." Valentina added as she threw her bag over her left shoulder and picked up Lola in her arms. Costanza reached out and hugged the two of them prompting Lola to lick her on the nose and make the older woman chuckle with glee. "Querida, mi casa es tu casa, enjoy it and do your work in peace, I like and trust you." They exchanged further goodbyes and Valentina walked out into a cool night with a very tired dog in her arms.

She set down Lola and they walked across the park slowly. The walk was prime time for Valentina to reflect on her day, which she found very relaxing to do. Thinking back to all Costanza shared with her today, what kept repeating in her mind was what she said about finding a true and honest love and fighting to safeguard it.

CHAPTER 11

The Witching Hour

Upon entering the bustling hotel lobby the concierge approached and discreetly informed Valentina that Diana Monroe was at the bar waiting for her. Valentina handed over Lola with instructions to the concierge and proceeded to glance at her image in a mirrored pillar. She touched up her lip gloss and ran her fingers through her hair then took a deep breath and proceeded to the bar wondering what this woman wanted with her. She was indeed unsettled and could only guess that Monroe's unexpected visit had to do with acquiring the apartment and expensive furniture and nothing to do with David. She walked calmly as if she had no cares in the world passing tourists and hotel employees.

Sitting alone against the red leather banquet in a corner of the bar sat Diana Monroe. She looked regal in her navy DVF wrap dress and knee-high boots. Around her neck was a casually knotted Hermes scarf with shades of blue, gold and red. Her glossy golden hair shone bright and gave off an air of majestic proportions. Valentina approached her confidently and could not help but admire the beauty of the haughty woman she was about to encounter for a second time. Both women stared at one another as Valentina spoke first, "Diana Monroe. We meet again."

"Hello Ms. Puig. Thank you for meeting me. I fear we got off on the wrong foot yesterday." She spoke in sugary tones that made Valentina more suspect of her intentions. Behind her steely blue eyes was a darkness that did not escape Valentina.

"I noticed you entered with a little dog. Do you always travel with it?"

"Sometimes, it depends on where I will be and for how long." Valentina offered curtly.

Chuckling, Monroe added churlishly, "How very Paris Hilton of you." This remark infuriated Valentina but she maintained a poker face.

Growing impatient and increasingly tense Valentina stated, "Let's get to why you have asked me here. I have had a long day."

"First, let's get some champagne." Before Valentina could protest, Diana rudely snapped her fingers and ordered a bottle of Cristal. She twirled her enormous diamond ring around her finger and watched Valentina with a grin.

Valentina would not show this woman any concerns and pretended to take her gestures and comments in stride.

"Are you celebrating something?" asked Valentina.

"Actually you are. We are going to be good friends as we have so much in common."

Both women watched one another with clear disdain as the waiter with much fanfare uncorked the bottle and poured the champagne carefully into two sparkling crystal flutes.

"You lost me there. We have nothing in common."

Diana Monroe lifted her flute prompting Valentina to do the same.

"To new friends and acquisitions."

Although they clinked glasses Valentina was perplexed at this cheer and ingratiating woman.

"I'll get to the point. I am prepared to make you a very wealthy woman. You see, I have to get this apartment for several reasons, one, is La Duquessa was a distant relative and that's a fun conversation piece. She was something like a fourth cousin and I have waited an eternity for her to die. Two, I admire the history of that space and its architecture and three I want it to become the European studio for my precious jewels acquisition company. You have an obvious "in" with that servant whose name escapes me now. If you are able to get her to sell the apartment to me I am prepared to equal the amount of the sale but in English pounds to you." She cocked one eyebrow when she suggested the amount in pounds.

At hearing this Valentina's eyebrows rose. She understood what Monroe's proposition meant. The apartment was valued at 5 million USD but in pounds that translated to a whopping 8.5 million dollars. For Valentina such an amount was beyond her wildest dreams and almost impossible to achieve in her lifetime. She kept a serious expression knowing that regardless of how attractive this amount was she would never betray Costanza.

"I doubt I can be of any help to you. Ms. Linares de Palacios lives there. It is her home. She never mentioned the apartment was for sale."

Diana Monroe drank more champagne and from her throat came a deep laugh.

"It is so refreshing to meet someone so naïve. Everything is for sale and everyone has a price. You help me and I will make sure you are taken care of for the rest of your life. What do you say, friend?"

Friend? What I really want to do is smack that smile off your face, you bitch, thought Valentina.

Here was a woman who had few scruples and assumed money could buy everything. Keeping her demeanor and responding calmly was difficult but Valentina added, "Perhaps you should go through my direct supervisor Marcus Napier. He would need to sign off on everything and could be more convincing with the current owner. I cannot help you."

Valentina raised herself to leave but Monroe placed her hand over her wrist causing her to sit down again.

"Marcus has been indifferent to me since my engagement. I think he's angry I have chosen a man younger than he. We were, until recently, friends with benefits but Marcus is not a man easy to control to my needs whereas my current fiancée I have right here," she pointed her index finger to the palm of her other hand. Valentina was starting to feel very uneasy with this woman who spoke so freely about her control of men and those she discarded like yesterday's newspaper.

Gathering her bag Valentina rose slightly to ease her way out of the banquet. Diana rose as well but remained standing proudly. Staring at one another Diana started to speak firmly, "You will support me won't you Valentina?"

"Support you? Never. I will not take a single step in helping you with anything."

The silent fury that lay beneath Monroe was evident in her eyes and tightness of her shoulders. She lifted her chin and declared loud enough for nearby tables to hear. "Are you forgetting that I am on the Board of Director's of Infinity Acquisitions? I will go back to the board and insist you be fired for insubordination." Monroe gave that same sweet smile that Valentina wanted to slap off a second time.

"You do what you have to do Monroe but not everything or everyone has a price. Thanks for the champagne." She turned to leave and could feel the woman's eyes cutting through her as she walked away proudly with a straight back and her head held high.

Valentina wanted to run from the selfish conniving presence of Diana Monroe. She felt dirty from having been near her and from what she just heard. Monroe's threats did not bother Valentina as much as what she implied about her relationship with Marcus. Marcus had lied to her. She felt foolish for thinking he was different and was eager to tell him off.

Upon entering the room she was welcomed with the floral arrangement Marcus had sent earlier. Valentina lifted the heavy vase and threw the bouquet into the trash. The flowers collapsed noisily into the large aluminum bin as water from the vase eased its way out from the bottom onto the carpet.

So you and that monster were friends with benefits. Screw you too Marcus. Valentina stared down at the flowers as she thought of Marcus and Diana as more than friends. She swallowed hard and went to shower to remove the stench of Monroe's expensive perfume and threats out of her head.

CHAPTER 12

Restraint

Marcus was in the store walking around and glancing at his watch. He always visited different departments to clear his head or when he needed inspiration. The iPhone had not rung with her call making him grow increasingly impatient. He walked right out the door and onto Broadway and over to the park where the kiosks were being set up for the Autumn Farmer's Market. He stopped to look at some dog food displays in the window of the Petco on the corner by Union Square. Glancing at his phone wasn't helping but he desperately needed to hear Valentina's voice. He decided to grab a coffee from the nearby Starbucks to relax. When it was obvious she wasn't calling he decided to take the initiative. The phone rang and rang and then went to voicemail. He wasn't leaving any messages so he got up, left his coffee and walked back to his office convinced that his past affair with Diana Monroe had turned off Valentina. Marcus wanted to explain how dating Diana Monroe had been a chore and difficult at times with her high maintenance demands and dull friends.

He called in his secretary Melanie and had her cancel his dinner with a magazine editor for a story about his rise in the company. He also called his housekeeper Sally and told her to go home early and tell Jimmy his driver to take the rest of the day off as well. Marcus wanted to get home and be alone. Service people mulling around tending to his needs would only cloud his mind and upset him.

Upon arriving, he walked into the kitchen for water and noticed that Sally had prepared a plate of salmon, vegetables and rice pilaf and left it on the warming plate on the stove. He grinned despite himself and proceeded to prepare for a workout. Today he wanted to push himself to the limits.

After a warm shower to soothe his aching muscles, Marcus leaned against the railing and stared at his tiny garden two flights below. New York townhouses were usually three flights of living space with small gardens and balconies. His phone rang and thinking it was Valentina he answered it hastily and said, "I'm so glad you called Valentina." To his surprise Diana Monroe purred on the other end, "Hi lover, if I weren't an engaged woman I would run right over and hop into your bed as I did many times before my darling Marcus."

At hearing her voice Marcus froze yet remained cool to play her game. He knew Diana Monroe and women like her all too well. Her type was conniving and opportunistic who used and discarded people as they went about obtaining what they wanted. He spoke with measured words, "Ah, it is you Diana, I mistook you for someone else. Why are you calling me at this late hour?"

"Late? Why Marcus we closed down many places with our partying, don't you recall how much fun we had?"

His patience was wearing thin. He kept his cool but used a stern tone, "I'm busy right now, get to the point Diana."

"Hmm, your manners have taken a hit my love. I am calling to advise you that the pretty brunette from your office, Valentina, has acquired several valuable pieces I am interested in for myself. I want you to see to it that she directs this sale to me at wholesale prices, not retail. Also, I need that apartment space. It is perfect for my new company and its central in Europe. Because it's Madrid I can get anywhere in an hour."

He heard her puffing on a cigarette as he swallowed all three ounces of his whiskey and felt every hair on his body bristle with anxiety. He immediately knew there was a problem because she was still in Madrid with Valentina.

"Not a chance Diana. She got there first and after you left those pieces have been sold to a private buyer. As far as I know the apartment is not for sale." He would rather die than tell her he himself had purchased the bedroom furniture as a gift to Valentina. Diana's tone became demanding.

"You owe me Marcus and remember I'm on the board therefore…"

If there was one thing he had zero patience for were condescending threats and attitude. Giving her a reminder of his temper, he snapped back, "Give up the act Diana, I owe you nothing and I don't give a shit that you are on the fuckin' board. Go ahead and tell everyone we dated, see if I give a damn. But don't you ever threaten me or call with your bullshit again. Are we clear?"

"Oh my goodness Marcus, you are so aggressive towards me. When you answered the phone you thought it was Valentina. How chummy and friendly you two are. Here's how this will play out my love. If you don't want me to make a lot of noise to have her dismissed get me what I want. It is obvious you have a thing for this woman but I already told her we ARE friends with benefits."

Diana Monroe's poison always managed to bring out his rage and the least favorable aspects of his character. He felt the whiskey rise up his esophagus and that usually followed his hitting or destroying something. Taking a deep breath and counting to three Marcus responded in measured words and a stern tone. "No, here's how this will play out Diana. You will stay the Hell away from Valentina Puig and I won't leak to the proper outlets your involvement in the hedge fund scandal that brought down your pals at Smith Barnes."

Monroe bristled at the threat Marcus spit back. She recoiled from her cell phone and gave a nervous giggle and changed her tactic.

"Oh Marcus, you can be so funny at times. All I want is for you to try to obtain those magnificent pieces and do your best to persuade the owner to sell the apartment. We have history my love and I only want what is best for you. Will you try my angel?" Monroe could feel her pulse race as she waited for his response.

Marcus pressed END on his phone having heard enough from a woman he had grown to dislike immensely. After staring at her phone Diana angrily smashed it into the gilded length mirror of her hotel room sending shards of glass crashing everywhere. She screamed and wept at Marcus bringing up her greatest fear of being arrested because of her involvement in the largest scandal of insider trading in United States history. Several of her associates were already behind bars and serving lengthy sentences. She was saved because she had her attorneys register her under an alias and launder her money through Chinese stocks but if the prosecutor had an inkling of her involvement she would be doomed. She poured scotch into a tumbler and sat hugging and rocking her shoulders.

Marcus called the fleet services and arranged for a flight to Madrid within the next two hours. Walking downstairs to his office he served himself another whiskey and stared out into the cold night and called Valentina. Again the phone rang and went to voicemail. He wanted this relationship more than he needed to breathe. For far too many years he desired Valentina from afar knowing that she had all the makings of a real friend, lover and wife. All he wanted was to make her laugh again and in recalling their first kiss his body tightened in desire. He daydreamed taking her body and devouring it with kisses and bringing her to that point where she screamed from ecstasy because he was the reason for her immense pleasure. But now Diana Monroe had poisoned her image of him and he had to be there to mend her heart before it permanently hardened against him.

Marcus raced upstairs and threw clothes into an overnight bag. He called a cab and instructed the driver to John F. Kennedy airport. The flight left as scheduled arriving in Madrid at 10 a.m.

Upon arriving it occurred to him that Valentina could be in any of the numerous hotels in this large city. Also, how would he find out on a Saturday with New York time being around 4 in the morning? Marcus found himself in a state of confusion he was not accustomed to. He stood with bag in hand in the middle of Barajas International airport not knowing which way to go. Pressing his assistant Melanie's number he waited for her to answer. At this early hour Melanie answered the phone groggily but it did not surprise her as it had happened several times before and it was in her job description. She too had no idea where Valentina could be found but suggested he give her a few minutes to contact Cece. To his relief Cece did remember the name of the hotel and shared it readily as she ate a McDonald's breakfast with two girlfriends after a night of partying at the trendy Vandal club.

Marcus went to a nearby coffee stand and ordered an espresso. He drank it hurriedly as he read the text from Melanie with the name of the hotel. A cab pulled up and he gave the name of the hotel to the driver in perfect Castillian. The day was sunny and bright and a sharp contrast to Marcus' dark and pensive mood, as he did not know what exactly to expect from Valentina. Upon entering the hotel, Marcus first inquired if Valentina was indeed staying there and when this was confirmed he requested a room with a view to the park on a high floor. The receptionist handed him a keycard and watched the tall elegant man briskly walk to the elevator banks. Valentina's room was two floors below his so he went there first. He rapped on her door gently at first and then with more force wondering if perhaps she was still asleep as it was Saturday. When no answer came he went up to his room and jumped into the shower.

Wrapped in a hotel bathrobe he walked out to the small wrought iron balcony to have a smoke. Marcus admired the well-tended and beautiful grounds of the park that stretched out before him. He inhaled slowly and stared ahead when he spotted Valentina running back with Lola along the edge of a curvy lake. A smile curled up to his lip as he stepped back into the room and removed his robe to dress. He raced to the elevator and ran out into the lobby where he saw Valentina walking in with Lola prancing by her side. Her eyes looked up in surprise and saw him looking directly at her with blue eyes that echoed fear, love and concern all at once. Valentina was too stunned to move. Marcus walked over and picked up the pup and kissed her amber colored cheeks and stroked her ears while never removing his eyes off Valentina. All he could do was wait.

"Good morning Valentina. I know Monroe has said things to you that I can assure you are wrong. All I ask is that you allow me a few minutes to put all my cards on the table and tell you everything, please."

Valentina looked around her and licked her lips.

"You owe me no explanations Marcus. Your friend with benefits explained everything to me and as far as I know I no longer have a job thanks to your girlfriend."

Her smoldering anger was all too real for Marcus. He was reaching but had to leap forward, "Let's not talk here in the lobby. Please just a few minutes of your time and if you think I'm still bullshitting then I will return to New York. I promise."

Valentina looked exasperated when she responded, "I am going up to my room to shower. I have a few things to do so why don't you just leave me alone. I'll finish this job and return to…" He put down the dog and swiftly took her by the shoulders and kissed her gently. Not caring that anyone was in the lobby he took her face in both hands and pressed his forehead to hers and whispered, "Just a few minutes, I beg of you."

Valentina broke away from his embrace and walked calmly to the open elevators and pressed her floor. He too got on and walked out with her and waited to be invited into her room. She left the door open and as he entered he was met with a waste bin filled with the flowers he had sent and a water stain on the carpet.

Marcus took a seat on a chair in the suite and watched as Valentina kicked off her running shoes and proceeded to wipe down and feed the dog. Then, without saying a word she entered and locked the door to her bedroom. He walked out a second time that morning to a balcony to have another smoke and could not help but think of ways he wanted to murder Diana Monroe.

Valentina stood under the shower not certain what to think. *On the one hand Marcus came all this way to clear misconceptions and on the other hand he had lied*, she thought to herself.

She let the water soothe her muscles but the shower was useless in clearing her head. Mixed feelings clouded her ability to think. She thought about the distance Marcus traveled all the way from New York and wondered if this meant his intentions were genuine towards her.

There I go again being a stupid romantic and setting myself up for more heartache. She firmly squeezed the excess soap out of the loofah and hung it on the peg in the shower. She also couldn't help but wonder if he was in cahoots with Monroe to get this apartment. These doubts were unsettling and infuriating to her.

After what seemed an eternity, Valentina came to the living room dressed in jeans, boots and a cashmere sand colored batwing sweater. She finger combed her moist hair and looked straight at Marcus who stood there like a chastised schoolboy. They looked at one another like two gunfighters ready to draw their weapons.

Walking to the balcony windows and crossing her arms across her chest, she said firmly yet quietly, "You have one minute to explain why you lied to me about your relationship with Diana Monroe."

Marcus rubbed his hands together and then ran them through his hair. His right hand reached out to Valentina but she stepped away.

"We started dating about a year after I lost my wife. At first it was just dating and then we became lovers and we were together for about two years. I broke it off with her when she started making demands that we should wed. Over the years I dated different women not unlike you dated different men…"

Valentina glared at him. She was livid he would include her in his messy tale of former lovers and sharply snapped, "Perhaps I dated different men but none of them were my fuck buddies!"

Marcus was taken aback at how deeply Valentina's words cut through him. Her eyes glistened with anger and also a sense of loss when he took two large steps forward and reached out to her but she moved sideways to avoid him. Marcus stood steadfast staring at the balcony windows. Not one to claim defeat easily and in a voice choking with anxiety and the fear of losing her without ever having her he said softly, "I apologize for that comment. I was not suggesting you were anything like Diana." He took two steps closer to where Valentina stood.

"Valentina, we can rehash and live in the past or we can start anew from this point, right here and now. You tell me. I have shared my feelings for you and with every passing moment my love for you grows. Everyone before you except my deceased wife meant nothing to me and while it's true that Diana and I reconnected over the years it was only for sex and nothing more. I haven't been with her in over a year."

He moved towards her and took her hand in his and led her to the sofa where she sat and closed her eyes as she rubbed the space between her eyes. She looked up at him as he gently moved her chin to look his way. Keeping her eyes downcast, Valentina feared looking up and getting lost in his sparkling blue eyes. She also feared those same sensual eyes might cause her body to betray her. Marcus kissed her cheek, then her eyelids and finally her lips. His arms encircled her gently as his mouth pressed firmly against hers. Her body started to feel warm and tingly in places that she knew she could not control. Reacting swiftly Valentina brought her hands up and took his face in them. She moved away enough to utter, "We will have to do this my way Marcus. I'm not jumping into bed with you and becoming your new friend with benefits. Give me space and time and more importantly, no secrets from this day going forward."

The muscles in his jaw twitched at hearing that term yet again from her lips but he knew he had to agree to her conditions. Breathing a small sigh of relief he asked, "Okay, but can we have some breakfast because I'm starving."

Without smiling she reached over to her cell phone to order breakfast, and while she waited for reception she asked him, "Where are you staying Marcus?"

"Right here, two floors above you."

"You didn't waste any time."

"Valentina, You are too important to me and I will prove it to you if it takes me a lifetime. But I really hope it doesn't take that long as I'm starving."

"Breakfast will be here in 20 minutes. Last night I had an uneasy conversation with that woman downstairs in the bar. She offered to pay me 8.5 million pounds if I convinced Costanza to sell the apartment to her."

"For Monroe that amount is pocket change. In full disclosure, I didn't have a cheery conversation either on the phone. She threatened to go to the board and have you fired but I had an ace up my sleeve that I am certain left her trembling with fear. I threatened her with disclosing her name in some unsavory investments if she did not leave you alone."

Valentina looked at her hands and said quietly, "Thanks, I guess."

Valentina moved further away from the sofa to get perspective on the situation. Marcus smiled at her and it was then that she noticed the dark circles under his eyes and the pronounced lines that crinkled at the corners. Despite these tell tale signs of exhaustion she liked what she saw. Without showing any interest at his rugged handsomeness, Valentina gave Marcus a halfhearted smile and watched as he slouched down on the sofa and rested his head. Within seconds she noticed he was asleep.

Valentina quietly cancelled the breakfast and went downstairs with Lola where she had a tea and croissant al fresco. An hour later upon returning she found Marcus stirring and opening up very sleepy eyes. She leaned over him and whispered, "Come let's go get a proper breakfast and then you can sleep the afternoon." He followed her much the way her dog does and he was grateful that for once he was not in command of a situation.

Outside they hailed a cab and went to a neighborhood café where they had a delicious potato omelette and grilled peasant bread with tomatoes. There was hardly any conversation as they tucked in eagerly into their meals. The strong café con leche perked up Marcus and it was then with the wind blowing her hair away from her face that he knew he was done for it. This woman filled every space that was vacant in his heart in much the same way his wife had except that this was so much more. Valentina promised a future, youth and vitality. Her vibrancy and natural beauty was a life sustaining elixir that he yearned to drink from. The flecks of gold that danced in her brown eyes brought a grin to his face as she watched him stare at her and wondered what was in his head. But it was important for her to maintain the aloofness that kept him at bay. She did not care if he suffered because he had lied. If she caved to those bewitching eyes and his sensuous mouth he might think her to be a weak woman who could be played for a fool.

They left the street side restaurant and walked along the quiet and deserted callejones or alleyways. There, he unsuccessfully attempted to reach out for her hand on several occasions but she ignored him or moved away. They pushed ahead and fell upon plaza after plaza until they were exhausted and on the other side of the park. Here, Valentina showed Marcus El Porton and its pretty fairy light courtyard. It was now about 3 in the afternoon and the warm sun took the chill out of the air. Many small shops and fancy boutiques were shutting down for siesta. The next two hours of siesta were about relaxing after a large afternoon meal and perhaps catching a nap. Major businesses had done away with this time honored way of life but a large part of the population maintained the tradition.

Passing statues, fountains and beautifully manicured promenades they walked along without saying much to one another. He yearned to embrace and fill her with kisses and so much more but he had to play by her terms. It was the price he had to pay for not being entirely truthful.

They went around the statue of the fallen angel and here was where Valentina stopped. She closed her eyes and made a wish. Marcus looked curiously at her but restrained from talking. They moved along until they reached the hotel. It wasn't until they were in the elevator when Marcus spoke up, "Will you follow the time honored tradition of napping the afternoon away?"

Valentina smiled and responded, "Sure I will, but alone. So why don't you go rest and I'll do the same in our respective rooms. This way we will both be nice and fresh for later."

Marcus chuckled at her retort and held the doors open for her as she stepped off her floor. Escorting her to her room he kissed her hand and asked with slight trepidation in his voice, "You aren't going to escape while I snooze, are you?" Stepping into her room she closed the door slowly as she coyly said, "I suppose that is a gamble you will have to take Mr. Napier."

He stood staring at her door and for a fleeting moment he considered camping outside on the carpet but thought this would seem too desperate a move. Instead he went to his room where he reordered the same floral arrangement sent to her room with the concierge. Not packing a suit he stood over his bed staring at the few pieces of clothing he hastily threw into his bag. There was a crisp white shirt, jeans, the leather jacket he wore all day and some T-shirts. Picking up his phone he called the Brioni shop in Barcelona and ordered a dark navy suit in his size, He instructed the tailor over the phone to check his online statistics for a perfect fit and to have it delivered within two hours. After enjoying a scotch he fell asleep and dreamt of making love to Valentina.

The evening was misty with a light rain falling while the sun fought to keeps its place in the sky. The ochre light danced on the sidewalks and glowed everywhere with such intensity that it gave Madrid a festive mood despite the light rain. During the early evening hours Marcus was showered and slathering cologne on his neck and chest. This evening meant a lot to him because he had to woo Valentina and if extremely lucky consummate their love. Although he knew making love to her was not likely as she was still uncertain and upset with him he did know he had to try to convince her to give their budding romance a chance.

The new suit had been delivered while he napped. After a quick inspection of his clothes he called Valentina and sent up a quick prayer that she would answer. A smile spread across his face as he heard her voice.

"Hi Marcus, did you have a restful nap?"

"Yes, actually it was quite rejuvenating. Did you enjoy your rest?"

"I did not nap. I had a lot on my mind and needed to think. So what plans do you have for this evening?"

Not liking the glibness in her voice he tried to sound cheerful although he was worried she might not want to let him take her out. He chose not to let her indifferent tone affect him too much and pushed ahead by sharing his plans.

"I would love your company for dinner. Are you in agreement?"

Valentina liked how he was not assuming she would fall directly into his arms and remarked, "Okay, sounds good. I am a bit hungry. Is it dressy or casual?"

"Well, let's make it a little dressy because we already did casual in New York. We are in Madrid after all. Does eight sound good to you?"

"I'll be ready. See you then."

Her abrupt ending and coolness was driving him mad with concern. To Marcus, Valentina's responses sounded like she was talking with a girlfriend. He longed for her sweet gentleness and to see those sultry brown eyes look upon him with desire. Waiting was difficult but he also understood that to win the game he had to be patient and play by the rules.

Outside her room Marcus cleared his throat before knocking. He rapped gently on the door and within seconds Valentina opened to reveal herself wearing a sleeveless, lace, cream mini dress. Her long toned legs looked magnificent and ended in a pair of Jimmy Choo pointed nude heels. Valentina had parted her chestnut hair off center and gathered it in a full and sexy chignon. With just earrings and a ring, she gathered her overcoat. Marcus stood there dumbfounded marveling at this stunning woman. With little to no makeup and minimal accessories she looked majestic. Noticing his expression that was a cross between admiration and shock she snapped her fingers in the air to bring him back to Earth. "Hey, are you going to stand there all night or would you like to help me with my coat?"

Noticing the way his suit fit him to perfection did not go unnoticed. She took in all of Marcus in his stark white shirt opened at the neck and silk light blue and yellow pocket square. For a few seconds they devoured each other with mutual admiration.

Marcus moved swiftly over to her and moved his large hands up her arms and looked purposefully at her face. She knew he was smitten because his eyes were wild with desire and his mouth was slightly open. Valentina wanted him to know she wasn't a woman to toy with. Her feminine wiles would drive him insane and she intended to play for a while. He went to kiss her when she jerked away and started to place her overcoat over her shoulders. He grabbed her forearms harder and this time he kissed her mouth. His tongue made love to hers and together they swam in each other's passion. Valentina did not fight, as she was rendered useless with his powerful arms holding her while his mouth explored hers.

I so want this right now but I can't. Damn you for kissing me so right and smelling so damn good, Valentina thought to herself as her body warmed up to his incredible kissing.

Pulling away they stared into each other's eyes saying things that only lovers can understand. Still holding her he whispered apologetically, "Sorry about your lipstick."

She was so intoxicated with his fragrance and the headiness of his kisses that she muttered, "Oh, it's an easy fix. Just give me a minute."

Moving towards the large mirror in the suite she reapplied her gloss and noticed tiny beads of perspiration on the bridge of her nose. She swiped them away with her forefinger and also noticed the warm, moist feeling between her legs. Ignoring her traitorous body she turned around and they left the room.

At Bogui Jazz Lounge they dined on tapas and mini paella Valencianas. Marcus shared his childhood with Valentina. She listened and asked questions about his mother and father and their relationship. Her eyes moistened when Marcus asked her about her parents. Valentina shared how much they loved one another and how empty and lonely she felt at times without them. She also told him about her vivacious Tía Carmela and how much she respected and loved her. When Marcus volunteered an interest in going to the Bronx to meet her aunt she asked dubiously, "Are you sure? I can't see a rich guy like you visiting a little old lady in the Boogie Down Bronx?"

Marcus laughed heartily at her reference to the Bronx's nickname and he added, "Oh my God, I haven't heard that in decades. When I was a kid in Junior High School we took turns trying to breakdance on the street and being one of the few white guys in my little "gang" I paled next to my black and Latino friends. I almost broke my neck trying that craziness." She laughed and teased him, "Awe, are you rhythmically challenged?"

Marcus heard the Mambo playing and stood up extending his hand. Valentina followed him to the tiny dance floor where to her surprise he moved gracefully with plenty of Latin flair and fervor. When the pulsating and sexy beat ended he pulled her against his body and whispered in her ear, "I have nothing that is challenged my love and if you let me I will show you."

To the sensual sway of the bolero they danced slowly grinding their pelvic areas together and looking deeply into respective blue and brown eyes. Valentina was aroused and warm and loving the way she felt in his embrace. He enveloped her entire being with a sense of safety and sensuality unlike anything she felt before. This man had her body floating and her head in a trance. Everything about Marcus was sensual.

His lips grazed hers as his tongue tickled her teeth and entered to a slow kiss where he explored her mouth while dancing to the slow beat of the intoxicating music. The music stopped and he embraced her tighter. His mouth gave her a small kiss on the lips and he escorted her back to the table to pay the bill and collect her coat.

The night was brisk but the post rain sky was clear and filled with faraway tiny stars. They walked for a short while and then hailed a cab to the hotel. Valentina's mind was racing. On the one hand she wanted Marcus to make love to her but on the other hand she needed to wait and make him wait as well. If any real relationship was to develop from this moment on it was important for Valentina to truly believe that Marcus was the one that she could trust for a lifetime. She believed in forever and in waiting for the one true love. The past experiences in Valentina's life had proved to her how deceptive men could be. She had decided that never again would she fall for cheating, lying men.

The cab dropped them off in the early morning hours of Sunday. They went up to Valentina's floor and to her surprise it was Marcus who made no efforts in further seducing her. He opened her door and walked her inside.

"It has been a very long day."

Valentina wanted him to stay but also fought against what she should do which was to sleep alone. She removed her coat and shoes and stood before him.

"Yes, this has been a very long day. Are you returning tomorrow to New York?"

Marcus walked over and played with her ear moving his index finger along the edge and gently squeezing her earlobe driving Valentina mad with desire.

"I am leaving tomorrow at noon. Valentina, I will respect you and give you the space and time you need because I love you."

He lowered his head and gently kissed her lips. In awe she stood there watching as he left her in her hotel room alone.

It was ten in the morning when Valentina called his room. Marcus was packed and ready to leave to the airport within the hour. He didn't want to leave her but she insisted on completing the job and acquiring all necessary data for the company. Clearing his throat he answered the phone, "Good morning beautiful. Restful night I hope."Valentina paced her room nervously at the thought of him leaving.

"Hi, how about some breakfast before you leave?"

Marcus smiled into the phone and responded readily, "I only have one hour to spare so will it be my room or yours?"

Valentina swiftly responded, "Come to me. I'm not dressed and tell me what you want to eat."

"Not dressed? How delicious." He heard her huffing on the other end and knew she was rolling her eyes. Laughingly he told her what he wanted. "Okay, okay. If they have Spanish omelets I want that, if not, then ham and eggs will do and tons of coffee."

The sound of her laugh was musical to Marcus. Valentina said goodbye and proceeded to order breakfast. Within minutes Marcus was knocking on her door. The dog barked at him and jumped up for a kiss. Marcus gave her one on the cheek and then looked Valentina up and down in her sky blue silk kimono robe with pale pink cherry blossoms painted throughout. How he wanted to undo the ties and wrap his arms within and feel her sensuous body in his hands.

The porter came in and rolled the elegantly appointed cart over by two chairs. Lola barked relentlessly scaring the man away as Marcus gave him a generous tip. Together they enjoyed their breakfast, remembered the fun they had the previous evening and glanced lovingly into each other's eyes. Marcus snuck ham to Lola making the little dog sit by his side the remainder of the hour. She noticed Marcus had developed a five o'clock shadow that was speckled with grey hairs here and there and thought how becoming it was on him. His sexy appearance in a long sleeve cashmere Henley and jeans made her desires rise. Brazenly she stretched her naked foot along the side of his pant leg causing him to stop eating.

"Woman, if you want me to lose my mind and make love to you right here on the sofa and miss my flight please continue that with your foot. Otherwise, I suggest you stop."

Valentina stopped but added coyly, "Hmm, you need an entire hour. That is very interesting."

She laughed sensuously and got up to play some music. He noticed how she had relaxed more around him and enjoyed the calm between them. The sexual tension was there and Marcus wanted nothing more than to tear that robe off of Valentina and devour her but he was not going to push. Instead, he had determined to drive her mad with desire by teasing her as she also tormented him. He figured he could play harmless games as well as she could.

He got up and walked right over to her and took her arm to pull her into him. He kissed her hard and moved his hands behind her to feel and squeeze her bottom. She ran her fingers through his hair and pressed his mouth harder into hers. They kissed, felt each others growing desire and then he pulled away with a very obvious bulge between his legs. Marcus took a deep breath and came closer to her taking her hand and kissing the inside of her wrist to say, "Be careful while you are here and come back to me Valentina. I can't wait much longer. I love the Hell out of you."

Valentina watched him leave and just as he reached the door she shouted, "Wait!" Running into his arms she hugged him hard and said, "I want to take a leap of faith but I'm scared you will be like the others."

Marcus moved stray glossy strands of hair away from her teary eyes and kissed each cheek. After another gentle kiss on her mouth he whispered, "There is nothing for you to fear anymore my love. I will make you mine and I will make you very happy. That is a promise because you are the one."

Valentina's tears spilled over and they hugged and kissed. Marcus rushed out to the airport and Valentina remained behind to complete her work and dream of a brighter future.

CHAPTER 13

Liar!

Out on the balcony after Marcus left to catch his flight, Valentina relived the kisses and words spoken from his lips. She believed that Marcus was the man she had always hoped for but cobwebs from her past of poor behavior by previous lovers and the most recent brutal betrayal by David invaded and clouded these thoughts.

Being at a crossroads in her life and choosing the right road meant taking an enormous leap of faith. Marcus excited her and offered new possibilities. For Valentina she felt there was too much honesty in his words and in his manner to seem like he was being deceptive as other men had been in her past. She also knew him for so long that she understood how he worked, what he liked and disliked. What Valentina wanted was to get to know him better as a man. She desperately wanted to take this leap and throw caution to the wind because she felt safe with Marcus in ways she had never felt in past relationships. The ardor was obviously there between them and instinctively she knew they would be passionate lovers. But more importantly she felt that he would always protect her.

Just then a chilly breeze made her wrap her robe tighter around her. Lola was looking out and barking at every dog she saw below. Starting to feel cold Valentina moved inside with the dog and closed the balcony doors.

She surprised herself when she realized that being back in New York by the end of the week was what she wanted more than anything else. To make this happen she would need Cece's assistance to achieve this. She moved from room to room looking for her cell phone until she found it wedged between the cushions of an upholstered chair in the living room. Marcus had sent her a text nearly a half hour ago and it read,

"I'm sorry if I hurt you recently but it is my one true desire and a promise that I will be loyal to you forever. I love you."

Smiling down at the phone she dialed Cece's number. The young assistant groggily answered the phone and mumbled, "OMG, twice in one night. This is NOT in my job description. OMG! First Mr. Napier's secretary calls me and now you. What's up boss?"

Valentina apologetically, "Sorry to wake you Cece but I was wondering if you would like to come out here for a few days?"

The news tore Cece out of her slumber and made her sit up in her bed with eyes wide opened. Remarking loudly, "What? Does the Pope pray? I can be there tonight boss! Oh my God I have to shop and pack! I don't have anything to wear…"

Cece continued to talk and huff so excitedly that she did not hear when Valentina tried to cut in several times.

"Okay calm down Cece, now listen carefully. Bring only a carryon with essentials, your passport and a change of clothes because you will buy great stuff over here. Book a room for yourself at my hotel and get here in one piece."

Cece calmer on the other end spoke softly while emphasizing every word, "You are the best boss ever. I will be grateful to you always for this opportunity."

Valentina dismissively remarked, "Yeah, okay, whatever. Just get here safely and in your temporary insanity please do not forget the passport. See you soon."

Very excitedly Cece continued, "Sure thing boss. I'm already packing. See you in several hours. OMG! Thanks again!"

Valentina laughed at her exuberance, "Sure, it will be fun and you are welcome. Bye now."

With this Valentina finalized the call and proceeded to get started with her day. For the remainder of the morning Valentina had a silly grin plastered on her face. Her eyes shone with new love and she started daydreaming of a life with this interesting man.

Cece arrived late Sunday evening in a whirlwind of excitement and wasted no time in pulling Valentina into boutiques. They enjoyed a paella dinner at a local Tablao restaurant where Cece feasted on flamenco dancing.

Everyday after they completed work with the new acquisition they strolled the streets of the famous city with its parks, plazas and history. Cece polished her wardrobe with more neutral tones and fine accessories. She marveled at everything and to Valentina's amusement she took a photo with every statue and famous landmark. Valentina had several packages from Galerias Preciados, one of Madrids premier department stores and several boutiques. She picked up a handsome Hermes scarf for Marcus and a bag for her Tía at a leather boutique within Corte Inglés, the department store that Valentina considered the Macy's of Madrid.

Spending time with Marcus urged Valentina to wrap things up within the week and head back to New York. She didn't want to run away anymore because her heart wasn't hurting as it did when she arrived. David had quickly become just another boyfriend from her past and she wanted to move forward. Life was bright and full of fresh starts. This was Valentina's fresh start. She felt empowered and for the first time in her life she wanted nothing more than to be back home to be in her own space to plan a new future.

The week became one of endless phone calls, emails and supervising the moving of the pieces to have them shipped overseas. Cece returned to New York with her endless new wardrobe, and tacky touristy gadgets such as tiny flamenco dolls and a poster of a bullfighter with her father's name as the famous matador. All these things she squeezed into a new set of Louie Vuitton luggage, a gift from Valentina, and was back to New York by Tuesday.

Marcus and Valentina were each very busy with their work. It was becoming a habit for her to wait on his call. He too had developed a little routine for their calls by settling into his favorite chair in his home office with a scotch whiskey. Excitedly he called her and when he heard her purr his name he uttered, "God I miss you." Valentina was tired but yearned to chat with this incredible man that had quickly settled in her heart.

"I miss you as well," she whispered into the phone.

"I could be there in a couple of hours but let me remind you about this time you said you need because I don't want you to say I'm being pushy." He took a leap of faith praying she would not say anything other than, yes.

Softly she uttered, "I'll be home Sunday. We should wait a little longer but you are quickly mending my broken heart."

Pressing his lips together he sank deeper into his chair. Her last words would have to be enough for now and like the gentleman he was he responded, "I just want your happiness so if it means waiting a little longer then so be it." These last words were coming off his tongue reluctantly. Marcus had already figured out to charter a jet that would put him in Europe in five hours. He inhaled from the cigarette and stared ahead as he sat alone in his empty townhouse.

Valentina spoke up hoping to sound confident and enthusiastic, "I'm going to visit the Prado museum in the morning then return to pack."

Clearing his throat and not able to sit comfortably with the growing desire in his pants he got up to walk around the ground floor. He tried to control the discomfort he felt at hearing her voice and not being able to fill her with his love. Coming out a little more roughly than he intended Marcus demanded, "Valentina, when you get back I want and need serious time with you. Do you understand?"

The tone in his voice made her heart race. She knew what he meant and she too desired him. Making love with Marcus was something she now fantasized about constantly. Despite her desire being as intense as his she also feared that it could be too soon. Everything about him made her body ring with desire and to feel his body on hers was a treat she longed to experience.

Nervously she giggled into the phone and joked, "Mr. Intensity, you are making me blush and I haven't had dinner yet. So tell me, what are you doing in the coming days?"

Changing the subject was just a way to ease the obvious sexual tension over the phone but Marcus was too experienced for this when he sighed, "What I will be doing is planning on how I will ravish you and make you delirious with joy. I always mean what I say and you are my one and only priority. And if you let me I will love you until my dying day."

The decisiveness in his words was a new sensation for Valentina whose former lovers were cool about commitments and life revolved around their immediate needs. Lola was now stretching and carrying her toy in her mouth. She padded over and laid a stuffed penguin at Valentina's feet. She picked up the penguin and threw the toy across the large room, which prompted Lola to race after it.

Marcus asked, "Have I scared you off?"

Quickly she answered, "Oh Marcus, not at all. I'm just wondering about the things you say. No other man ever spoke so honestly to me and I long for a love that is honest, real and passionate. But I'm 35 years old and I want a family. I need to know if this is something you want as well?"

This conversation was best in person but Valentina had little time to waste biologically and her patience had run out with men. Her questions with Marcus would be as direct as the things he said to her. This was the sort of man he was and she knew he appreciated direct and honest people.

Before he answered he drank down two more ounces of whiskey hoping it would take the edge off his nerves. Valentina hit a real nerve when she mentioned children. Marcus had wanted children with his wife but her passing made that impossible. The other women he had met in the past years were all concerned with being wined and dined or interested in what they could get from him. Diana Monroe had her own wealth but she was extremely demanding and too spontaneous and selfish for Marcus' taste. He liked calmer women who enjoyed a Sunday in pajamas reading the paper or flipping through magazines. Marcus wanted a real life and not one that seemed like an endless cocktail party.

Exhaustion and a strong buzz hit Marcus hard after three scotches. Climbing back up the stairs to his room, he unceremoniously stretched himself across his massive bed and closed his eyes to respond, "I always wanted kids Valentina but my wife died and I did not notice any maternal desires in other women I met since. I want a family. I need a family. We already have a dog so I think that's one step in the right direction."

They laughed. It was time to go and she knew this as she heard the grogginess in his voice.

"We will chat later. Oh and Marcus, thanks for your honesty. I love this about you. Go sleep, okay?" Marcus closed his eyes and whispered, "And I love everything about you. Sweet dreams." He pressed end and let his mind and emotions take him to his youth when his father passed away from advanced Parkinson's disease and in recent years his mother. He was very much alone in this world and he, like Valentina, longed for family.

It was late October and although the air was brisk it was pleasant to walk around because the sun was warm and the leaves on the trees glistened. Madrid is a city filled with great boutiques and endless cafes. People move along without any care on Saturdays and Sundays. These two days were contemplative for Valentina. After her last chat with Marcus about building a family she was floating on air from hope for the future.

By Thursday, Costanza called Valentina. "I'm coming back tomorrow Valentina. Is everything going well?" she asked.

"Costanza, things are going smoothly. And I have to thank you for it because I have been here everyday for hours and was able to do it all without interruption. Thank you so much for the keys to the house and your trust," Valentina happily shared. The plan was that by Sunday she would be flying home two weeks ahead of time. With Ceci's help she was done in Madrid with just minor things to address.

"I am so glad," chimed Costanza. "Bueno, we will talk more when I return. Let's have dinner at Castiza. It's a very traditional restaurant near the apartment. There we can finalize everything," added Costanza.

"But only if you let me treat you," chirped Valentina.

"How sweet you are, thank you," Costanza said laughing. The women ended their conversations amicably setting eight thirty as a time to meet.

Valentina headed to her hotel room, ran in the park with Lola and showered. She was heading to the closet when she noticed her cell phone buzzing. She removed the towel from around her wet hair and as she finger combed the long brown tresses she pressed the phone on and listened to a voicemail from David. His voice was tremulous, angry and slurred. He obviously had had too much to drink or was high.

"Hey, Vale, why do you have to be such a vindictive bitch? My fiancé called me really upset that you took her chance away at some things she wanted. She found out how, I don't know, you and me had a thing and now she wants to cancel the wedding. Wow, you really are a piece of work. If you ever cared for me you would not do this to me "

She could not hear anymore because it was all so stupid and childish to her. This bothered her enough though to make her lose her appetite. It was about three in the afternoon in New York. Valentina felt she had to call Cece and inquire about how things were over there. Her assistant answered the phone immediately, "Valentina, hi how are you today?"

"I'm okay Cece, just called to find out if all was alright with the final details I sent to you."

"Sure, we have all those shipments ready to arrive by mid November. Everything is in place regarding shipments and a ridiculously BIG check is heading over to the lady who sold all these pieces. There is a lot of buzz about a big time display on the third floor on this period. Mr. Napier is very busy getting everyone on board. Girl, you worked fast, with my help of course," laughed Cece into the phone. Valentina took it all in and said, "Okay, well it sounds like you have it all under control."

"Oh yeah, guess what? I saw that Diana Monroe. She's not all that let me tell you. You put that girl in sweats and she's just another bottle blond." Cece laughed at her own comment but Valentina needed to ask, "When and where did you see her?" Gulping down an iced coffee Ceci took her time to say, "She came in yesterday and had a meeting with Mr. Napier. They were in his office for a long while and then they left together. When they were waiting for the elevator I saw her throw her arms around him and kiss him on the lips. He did not return to the office, so who knows."

Valentina's stomach felt cold and sick. She thought about how that woman was there and that they kissed. Feeling betrayed and furious she did not make any effort to suppress it, "Cece, think back and tell me exactly everything you know." Cece thought it was natural for Valentina to wonder about the woman who had stolen her boyfriend.

"Okay, she was here around 1p.m. Melanie looked really nervous because we could see Mr. Napier pacing back and forth in his office. Why do you ask?"

Valentina quickly dismissed herself, "Thanks Cece."

Cece was met with silence from the other end and wondered what could be happening but she had too much to do and also knew that when Valentina was upset it was best to not bother her for some time.

Valentina threw the phone on the bed and walked over to the window. She thought back to the intense conversation she and Marcus had had about family, love and building a future. It wasn't possible for Valentina to wrap her head around the fact that Marcus did not tell her that he had been with Monroe in his office and then left the store with her and did not return. She was not surprised that Monroe would go whining to Marcus but it was his keeping this from her that hurt her deeply. She felt deflated again and cried into her hands. Recalling when Marcus told her that he would sooner die than hurt her turned her tears to frustration.

He's just like all the other fools I have wasted my time with. No more! I'm done with you too Marcus. Valentina said out loud to herself as she walked back into the bathroom to rewash her tear soaked face.

The sunny day just turned gray and bleak. It was four in the afternoon when Marcus called her. She did not answer even though he tried two other times. On his third attempt he left a voicemail, "I have tried you several times Valentina. Just wanted to talk and hear your voice. I also want to tell you something that happened. Call me, I miss you so much." She turned off the phone without listening to his voicemail.

Nothing more happened for Valentina on Friday expect mulling around the hotel suite and waiting for her evening dinner with Costanza.

Men turned to look at the statuesque brunette as she entered the small restaurant. Valentina looked gracious in a sleeveless black dress with tall black boots. She stood elegantly and looked down the long bar filled with patrons. She had gathered her shiny hair into a side ponytail and had some gloss and mascara on to look polished. Costanza rose and they embraced one another and kissed on both cheeks. Costanza immediately noticed the withdrawn and sad look in Valentina's eyes. She wanted to probe but waited. They ordered wine and small dishes of tapas of seafood on crackers, cheeses and ham.

Restlessly Valentina asked Costanza, "I have been wondering what you will do now that the apartment is practically empty." Costanza wanted to chat about personal things but Valentina wanted to talk business. "Well, my home has grown too big for me. This apartment is too much space for an old woman without family of her own. I never intended to keep it so I will sell the apartment."

From the moment she entered the space Valentina loved the apartment. In this space she had allowed herself to daydream living there, throwing fabulous parties and swaying in loving embrace with Marcus. It saddened Valentina to think it would belong to someone else besides Costanza. "It would be sad to see you sell it and for this magnificent space to belong to someone else, who will likely tear down walls and put the kitchen in the living space," said Valentina glumly as she stared at her wine.

"Has Diana Monroe approached you or sent someone to speak with you about selling the apartment?" Valentina asked after drinking the remainder of the rich bodied red wine.

"Ha, as if I would sell anything to that wasp." Costanza's remark pulled a tiny grin onto Valentina's face.

Costanza was concerned to see Valentina so grim and dejected prompting her to take a chance at being nosy, "Tell me, since I last spoke with you what has happened? You told me everything was going smoothly. Has that ex boyfriend bothered you again?"

It was hard for Valentina to open up about herself but her aunt was too far and here was this woman face to face who would not judge her and showed genuine concern. Like a waterfall Valentina opened up to her and shared her budding relationship with Marcus. She went at length about the visit Diana Monroe made to his office and their kiss. Tears welled in her eyes as she told Costanza about the conversation she had shared with Marcus about a family and finally David's rude voicemail. As she spoke, the waiter interrupted and took their orders. Costanza listened attentively as Valentina shared how she felt deceived all over again and took her hand when the tears that threatened to fall choked her words.

Valentina added, "I'm leaving Sunday morning and don't know what I'm going back to."

Costanza ate quietly and noticed Valentina had not eaten much at all. Putting her utensils down she wiped the corners of her mouth and spoke up, "You are accusing this Marcus of things that are only in your imagination. David is an imbecile, we know that, but if Marcus has told you all those important things and expressed wanting a family with you what difference does it make that he spoke with Diana Monroe? Think about it, perhaps they left together but went separate ways outside. Perhaps she kissed him and he did not return the kiss. I would be careful if I were you to accuse a man like Marcus who has expressed his love to you."

Valentina was surprised she sided with Marcus. It upset her that Costanza did not understand the hurt she felt. She responded curtly, "Why should I give him the benefit of doubt if he hasn't told me of this "meeting" between them? Why should I be the one to always bend to make others comfortable?"

Valentina was too upset to hear much more but Costanza took the moment to add, "So why go back so soon? Stay here longer and see what happens."

Valentina thought about it. "Maybe, I don't know. I wanted to go to Barcelona for a few days and be back where my parents were from. You may be right."

The older woman remained quiet and just ordered a tea while Valentina had more wine. They finished their meal;

Valentina paid the bill and said their goodbyes. She shared with Costanza her address in New York and welcomed her to stay for a visit. Before they went separate ways Costanza asked, "If you go to Barcelona, where would you stay?"

Valentina knew she wanted to visit the beach. "I would stay in Barceloneta, most likely. The beach is there and although it's cold Lola and I love to walk on the beach when it's not summer. I know I'm weird," Valentina chuckled lightly.

Costanza smiled and really liked this woman who could laugh at herself yet hurt so deeply. They said their farewells and Valentina walked the long way across the park and felt her phone buzzing in her pocket. She looked at the screen and to her shock Diana Monroe sent her a selfie showing Marcus embracing and kissing her with his back to the phone. Valentina stared at the photo and recognized the elevator banks and knew it was at Infinity. She knew it was Marcus because she recognized his back and haircut. Diana's eyes, forehead and lustrous blond hair were clearly seen off to the side receiving an obvious kiss on the mouth. It was a confirmation that burned a hole in Valentina's heart. She determined at that moment to never believe Marcus again and forwarded the photo to him with a brief yet powerful text, "*LIAR!*"

Valentina walked back to her hotel room and let enormous tears fall while feeling defeated and foolish for trusting once again.

CHAPTER 14

Taking Flight

Armendariz Car Rental was just three blocks from the hotel and very accommodating. They gave Valentina a special harness that would secure Lola along for the ride to Barcelona. The porters helped pack the car while she paid her hotel fee and thanked everyone. Valentina bought water for the five-hour drive and chocolate. She walked Lola for an hour and played with her in the park to give her a chance to tinkle all over the place. Driving the standard Audi S8 along route NII/E90 towards Zaragoza was simple for Valentina as she was able to drive standard and automatic cars. She would later connect with the A2/E90 leading towards Lleida before reaching Barcelona.

Taking a flight would have cost about 50 Euros and taken one hour but Valentina wanted to get out of her head and drive. Driving was relaxing for her and especially so because she was familiar with this route having traveled extensively throughout Spain. She plugged her iPhone into the charger and opened the Pandora App to the John Mayer station. For the next couple of hours she listened to singer songwriters as Lola slept in the passenger seat. It was just after noon on Monday and she had three hours to go before arriving in

Barcelona. The iPhone had three voicemails from Cece, and two from Marcus along with numerous failed attempts at contacting her throughout the previous day. It was wrong not to return the calls but she needed space and this drive would give her as much.

Marcus walked over to Cece and asked point blank and nervously, "Where is she?" Cece remained seated and looked up at the tall, well dressed but very serious man and said, "She has not returned my calls or let me know of any further plans. The hotel did say she left but were not at liberty to share her whereabouts." Marcus said a quick, "Thank you," and walked away to the other side of the floor where his office was located. Within minutes he had secured a seat on a chartered jet and was heading home to pack. Before leaving he advised Melanie of the following, "Cancel all appointments until Wednesday. I may return Thursday but I will call you on Wednesday."

Melanie's eyes flew open because Marcus had arrived not thirty minutes ago and he was leaving in a hurry. She went about the business of canceling numerous meetings, lunches and dinners for her boss and was left to wonder what just happened.

A yellow taxi stopped in front of the store to drop off a passenger and Marcus quickly jumped in. As the taxi maneuvered through intense morning traffic on 6th Avenue Marcus heard a chime indicating a message or photo coming through on his phone. He glared at the photo and cursed Monroe out loud causing the driver to look into his rearview mirror. He immediately ordered the driver to take him to 735 5th Avenue. His next move was to call Diana but he took a deep breath to calm the anger that had built into an avalanche of hate for this woman. The word Valentina had typed was tattooed on his mind and he was determined to correct this come what may but first he had to deal with Diana and her dirty little game. As the taxi made its way to Fifth Avenue

Marcus left Valentina a text that he hoped would somehow clear misconception.

I left you an earlier voicemail saying I had to tell you something. You can't run away when we need to clear the air. That photo is complete bullshit and I will prove it to you. It's not right that you ignore me this way and assume I'm just like every other guy who has wronged you. Call me, please.

Arriving at the elegant apartment building he walked right in and did not announce himself but jumped into a waiting elevator. The uniformed doorman recognized him and resumed sorting the packages that had been delivered earlier. Arriving at her apartment the doors of the elevator opened to find Diana standing talking on her phone and holding a cocktail in the other hand. Her blue eyes registered surprise and concern to see Marcus. She quickly ended the call. They stared at one another and it took enormous control from Marcus not to squeeze her skinny neck until it snapped. Instead of resorting to obvious displays of fury Marcus decided to play along with Diana. He opened his arms in an embrace and hugged her warmly. Diana smiled and offered a kiss but he moved back and took the cocktail instead stating, "It's a bit early to drink even for you."

Diana tried to look casual but her anxiousness showed through. She shifted to the picture window with a vast view of Central Park and made small talk.

"Soon that silly Thanksgiving parade will be coming through and all those people crowding the front of the building. I have to make arrangements to be out of town. Can I convince you to come to Monte Carlo with me that weekend?"

Marcus moved slowly towards her and said calmly, "I think I already have a commitment for that weekend besides we aren't together any longer and if I am correct you are engaged to David Harrington. What would he say to this brazen invitation?" Diana hated to feel like a cornered rat. She could sense the smoldering anger behind his eyes. Taking a step away back towards her elevator door she offered a nervous explanation, "Oh him, well, I may have moved impulsively on that man. I guess I was just trying to make an old lover jealous and he was so interested in me that one thing led to another. Anyhow, things are heading south quickly with David as I have come to realize he is not for me after all."

Marcus was tired of the nonsense and gave up being civil. His statement was pointed and threatening, "I warned you before that if you interfered with my life I would not think twice about contacting a certain prosecutor regarding your involvement in that scandal."

Diana's face blushed brightly out of anger. She took an expensive cut crystal paperweight off the table in the foyer and flung it at Marcus. He caught it and placed it on a nearby surface and moved swiftly towards her grabbing both arms and shaking her until she cried out.

Desperate for his release she pleaded with Marcus, "Stop! You are hurting me! If I see one bruise I will run to the hospital and have you arrested for battery. How would that look for you Marcus? The mighty and elegant Mr. Napier with his sterling reputation suddenly arrested for hitting a woman." He released her quickly.

Rubbing her upper arms she spit out, "I have something on you too Marcus. You and that woman are together and that is against company policy. Those are grounds for dismissal for both of you." She looked at him smugly.

"Stay away or you will be wearing designer stripes in jail. I promise you Diana. You know I always keep my promises."

Marcus moved towards the door. Before he pressed for the elevator she was by his side holding his arm. She pleaded with him one last time in a gentler sugar coated voice that he knew all too well, "Marcus, my darling, we mustn't fight like this. Let's forget the entire thing and I will text your precious Valentina and apologize for my little indiscretion and you will forget about threatening me with that other thing, do we have a deal?"

Marcus glared at the woman he once thought he loved and saw how pathetic and manipulative she was. Pressing for the elevator he moved inside when the doors opened. The doorman had come up with Diana's mail. Marcus took this opportunity to use the doorman as a witness of a friendly farewell between he and Diana in the event she would want to spin this story in her favor. Extending his hand Marcus added, "I wanted to apologize for not giving you an opportunity to announce me earlier. I just came to pay Ms. Monroe a quick friendly visit."

The nervous doorman looked at Diana and then at Marcus and stated, "I don't understand, I just wanted to deliver the mail to Ms. Monroe. Mr. Napier you are still on our list below for not needing introductions, sir."

"Good, then all is settled. Please hold the door as I say goodbye one last time to my friend." The doorman nodded and held the doors opened as Marcus went over and blocked her body with his massive shoulders. He leaned down pretending to give her a kiss on the cheek but whispered in Diana's ear, "You had better pray Valentina understands or else. Don't you ever come between me and my life again."

The steely silence and hate in his eyes meant she was in trouble. Diana moved away from the elevator doors that proceeded to close and took her phone to text Valentina an apology.

Sorry to put you out earlier with that selfie. Marcus and I did not kiss. It was all a little joke, LOL.

Once home Marcus packed casual clothes into a Tumi suitcase, gathered his toiletries and called Jimmy. "Meet me outside in a half hour, we are going to Kennedy airport."

"Sure Mr. Napier, right away," came the response of the driver. Marcus grabbed his phone charger, his iPad and threw that into the case as well. He opened his safe where he kept his passport and money. Worried with thoughts he developed a monumental headache and tight shoulders. He wondered what he would encounter in Spain. All he knew was that Valentina was hurt and if he were not forgiven then Diana Monroe would pay dearly for her indiscretions.

The noisy traffic on the Van Wyck Expressway that led to Kennedy airport crawled. Marcus was livid and restless in the passenger seat and Jimmy could feel the fury coming off of his boss. The highway opened up as they left the endless construction on the road and approached the airport. With five minutes to spare he sprinted to the terminal and bypassed all the usual airport security details by flashing his private jet pass. He thought of how thankful he was to be in shape and not arrive winded. In the small executive plane he joined two other men who wore business attire like him and a young female attorney. A steward secured his luggage and coat. Marcus went over to shake hands with the other men and acknowledged the woman but took a seat far away as he was not in the mood to talk. He took off his jacket and settled into a very comfortable leather seat. Within minutes they took off and an attendant was bringing over a chilled vodka gimlet. He did not want to think about Valentina's silence but he was definitely concerned. He was sick with worry that she had determined never to deal with him again after Monroe's rude selfie. Throughout the six-hour flight he pretended to sleep to avoid conversation and refused any further food or drink.

Valentina arrived at the Mandarin Oriental and pulled up to the entrance. Immediately porters helped take her bag as she handled Lola who was restless and obviously in need to relieve herself. Valentina told the porter to leave her bags at reception and that she would return shortly. She looked around for green spaces and found a busy street with handsome buildings but no grass anywhere. They walked a few blocks as the dog tinkled and marked her territory and finally relieved herself. Valentina quickly scooped up the waste and deposited it in a waste bin on the corner. They walked back to the hotel where Valentina checked in and followed the porter up to the junior suite. Once there she kicked off her boots and lay down on the bed to check her phone. She called Cece and the call connected immediately, "Hi Cece, you called yesterday?" Cece spoke quietly to not alert anyone else, "I'm going to your office for privacy, hold on." Valentina waited as Cece unlocked the door and went to the windows.

"Okay, where are you?" Cece demanded to know.

"I'm in Barcelona," said Valentina wondering about the need for secrecy.

"Well, earlier today Mr. Napier came over to me and stared me down demanding to know where you are. I said I did not know and he walked away so pissed off but at least he did say, thank you." Cece added

"Oh really, well, I was having phone issues in Madrid." She lied to avoid telling her assistant anything personal. "I'll be back in a few days."

"Wait a minute…is everything okay with you over there, I mean I thought this deal was all wrapped up?"

"Yes, it is but I just need a little breathing space and wanted a few days to myself. Does Melanie know anything about Mr. Napier?"

"She's as confused as I was until now," huffed Cece into the phone.

"Cece, don't share with anyone where I am, if anyone should ask don't lie but say I have asked you not to share my whereabouts. I want to be left alone for a few days, okay? I should be back by Friday. Thanks Cece."

"Sure, no problem, be safe and see you soon." Cece added.

The call ended and Valentina thought about Marcus and how Cece said he was angry. She only recalled him being angry one other time when a new buyer lost a huge acquisition and even then Marcus took the nervous young man under his wing and personally re-trained him. But she remembered him raging in his office. She checked her text messages and saw the one Marcus had sent. Her first inclination was to delete it but instead she read it.

After reading the text she was angry and confused but realized she may have jumped to conclusions. Feeling tired and confused with all these developments she threw down the phone. She decided to have lunch at the pretty and airy restaurant downstairs just to get a little distracted and eat some food, as she was hungry after the three-hour drive. The Oriental Mandarin was a gorgeous hotel with impressive carved colonnades at the main entrance. Once inside it was tastefully decorated in whites and grays and so much greenery that the air was fresh and clean. She loved Barcelona and felt at home here as she did in Madrid or New York City. The only difference was that compared to landlocked Madrid, Barcelona has a famous port and beaches.

At the beautiful restaurant the Blanc Grasserie and Gastrobar, Valentina ordered a fruit and lobster salad with Riesling and devoted herself to people watch. As in major cities in Europe, people were all well dressed and good looking. She did not notice anyone overweight or sloppily dressed. It is true that at swanky hotels you might only see wealthy folk who are fit and can afford luxuries such as cooks and personal trainers but Valentina felt that everyone should make an effort to look their best at all times. Once she was sated she walked over to the spa and booked a manicure, pedicure and massage with hot stones. They would see her in one hour and this gave her plenty of time to go upstairs feed the dog and unpack. Valentina showered, dressed in a neat white tee shirt, grey slacks, ballet flats and wore no jewelry. She plugged her phone and saw Diana Monroe's text. She stood there shaking her head wondering to herself if this woman was still in high school given her immaturity. The text did serve the purpose of making Valentina rethink her earlier decision about Marcus. Despite the text she was so done with this third rate behavior that she put it out of her mind and turned off the phone.

Downstairs she requested that in two hours a gentle dog walker, no tugging at the leash, walk her dog. A generous tip was left and she proceeded to the spa.

The early evening hours found Valentina in a very relaxed dream like state as her muscles were worked to submission. The reflexology massage did wonders for her head and the pedicure and manicure made her feel polished and pretty. Once upstairs, she threw her clothes to the side and snuggled into the King size bed with Lola and fell asleep.

Marcus arrived at El Porton with luggage in tow and in a very foul mood after the hotel would not give him a clue as to Valentina's whereabouts. He was taking an enormous chance that perhaps Costanza would know where Valentina was staying. He pressed the bell and the short butler answered and invited him into the foyer and immediately he understood why Valentina was so enamored of this apartment. It was simply gorgeous in an old world style with architecture, carvings and moldings no one designed any longer. He was most impressed by its size. The butler took his coat and set his suitcase aside and asked him into the sitting room that was now empty except for two chairs and some fireplace tools. Costanza came hurriedly over to him and introduced herself.

"Ah, Mr. Napier. What a surprise to meet you here in Madrid. My name is Costanza."

"Good evening and please accept my apologies for not having an appointment with you and coming over unannounced."

"No problem, come, I only have this chair and the dining room to offer you to sit so we can talk."

"The chair is fine." Marcus made a mental note to relax because he could feel his own tension rising.

"What brings you to Madrid? Is everything okay with the pieces?"

"Everything is fine with the acquisition and let me take this opportunity to personally thank you for making us exclusive agents to such extraordinary pieces. They are beautiful and unique."

"Oh my goodness, I am so happy. It was such a pleasure working with that extraordinary lady, Valentina. She was magnificent."

He shifted in his seat at the sound of her name and asked, "Actually I am here because she has me worried. I cannot locate Valentina and was hoping you would know."

Costanza looked at Marcus carefully. She liked that he was so educated and classy as well as incredibly handsome. She thought he had the most radiant blue eyes she had ever seen. She asked, "May I be blunt Mr. Napier?"

"Please, ask or say what you will."

"Valentina came with a broken heart to Madrid and then she became so excited and happy because she was hopeful about you but then something happened and that poor girl was devastated once again."

She watched how his look at once became alarmed and curious. Opening his heart to a stranger was not a part of his personality but Marcus was bursting for information about the woman he loved. Sounding earnest and a little desperate he said, "Costanza, I love Valentina and would marry her today if she would let me but I need to find her. I have an idea of what has hurt her but I have no way of knowing where she is right now."

"Hmm, she learned of your meeting with that snobby Diana Monroe and something about a kiss and how you two left the office and never returned."

Marcus put his hands into his head and Costanza was tempted to console him but she refrained and waited. Marcus sat up, took a deep breath and said to Costanza point blank,

"Nothing happened between us. That evil woman sent her a photo that gives the appearance we were kissing when it wasn't so. You know where she is don't you?"

It was Costanza's turn to breathe deeply as she told Marcus, "I have become fond of Valentina and if your intentions are true I will tell you, otherwise I insist you leave her alone." The last words were spoken firmly.

His response came fast, "I believe that after her father, I am the only man who has truly loved her. My life without her is pointless. Please tell me where I can find her, I promise you, I will take care of her always."

Costanza looked him up and down and said, "She said she was driving to Barcelona, specifically Barceloneta. She would have arrived earlier today but I do not know which hotel."

It was late and he needed to find a place to stay.

"Thank you so much Costanza. I promise to contact you as soon as I have located Valentina."

"But do you have a place to stay?" She had to ask as his suitcase was parked in her foyer.

"No actually I do not." He said restlessly.

Costanza opened her arms widely and offered,

"Well, if you are not put off by staying in a simple but clean servants room you can stay here tonight if you like. It will be free of charge and you can start your search for Valentina tomorrow morning. What do you say?"

"I am indebted to you Costanza in more ways than one."

"Yes you are, so let's get you situated and then you will have a good meal. No excuses, no restaurants, you eat here. You look hungry."

Marcus was in no mood to argue and gratefully went to settle into his room. He tried Valentina's phone once again and when it went to voicemail he decided not to leave a message. After his meal of herbed roasted chicken with potatoes and sautéed spinach he felt calmer and stepped out to the terrace to enjoy a Spanish Ducado cigarrito. He marveled at the size of the terrace as he walked its length. The view of Madrid was spectacular with the impressive El Parque Del Buen Retiro looming below. In New York City this size space was unheard of especially in new architecture. *Wow,* he thought, *this apartment is magnificent.*

The butler brought over a scotch on a small silver tray for Marcus and bid him a goodnight.

CHAPTER 15

At Last!

Valentina awoke refreshed and feeling quite optimistic about her life. Noticing the numerous attempts by Marcus to reach her weakened her earlier resolve to move to categorize him as just another cad. There was something about him that just screamed loyal and honest. She knew that witch Diana Monroe was awful but to send a selfie that could destroy a relationship was low. Even getting her pathetic apology for the tasteless selfie was enough to convince Valentina that this woman was dangerous and never to be trusted.

While she took a cool shower and put on running gear she decided that at the very least Marcus should explain recent actions. That hopeful feeling was back and with that she dialed his number as she drank some coffee. Just when she realized the time in New York was three in the morning she went to end the call when he answered.

"Finally, it took you long enough to return my calls." He tried to sound lighthearted but he was too tense.

"I needed space, remember. Also, in light of recent events you are fortunate I'm giving you a call back." She tried to sound casual but it came out more guarded than she wanted.

"Valentina, I need to know, where are you?"

His voice sounded strained and it pained her because she knew he was worried. She wanted to hear his explanation and said, "I drove to Barceloneta and then over to the Mandarin Oriental for a few days. You don't sound sleepy, why are you up, isn't it around three in the morning?"

"Yes, it is three a.m. in New York but I am here in Madrid staying with Costanza in her amazing apartment. I am here for you Valentina and I am logging in lots of sky miles running after you. Seriously my angel, I am here to clear more misconceptions."

At hearing that Marcus was in Madrid Valentina felt hope rise again in her heart. No other man ever went out of his way to ease concerns or fight for her. Feeling confident she said, "Come to Barcelona because I want full disclosure of what went on between you and that witch, otherwise, go home." Her voice was strong and decisive.

"You will get a full account. I will take a local flight over and see you as soon as possible. I can't believe that in no time at all I will kiss that incredible mouth of yours." Marcus was throwing things back in his bags hastily as he spoke to her.

She was quick and added, "First it's business then we shall see. I have made some decisions about my life and I intend to carry them through."

"Sounds good to me. Just don't move, please Valentina."

"I am going for a walk on the beach and then returning to the hotel. I will see you soon." She ended the call.

She sounded all business and this disturbed him. He only liked that tone on her when she was conducting real business with others but with him the seriousness in her voice unnerved him to his core. Marcus wondered if he would have to pay for all her past boyfriends indiscretions. He was too old for mind games and intended to let Valentina know this today. He picked up his things and walked out to find Costanza and thank her for her hospitality and help. She hugged him and whispered in his ear, "Don't let her get away. She's very special." When he pulled back he noticed her eyes were wet. He figured that Costanza and Valentina had really bonded and appreciated her advice just the same, "I won't let her get away, I promise. Costanza, thank you." He left by giving her a kiss on the hand and an embrace. Costanza thought how chivalrous and rare to see this in a modern man.

The sound of the waves fed Valentina's soul and relaxed her. After they walked, Lola rolled all around the sand. They played for a long time and returned to the hotel exhausted and in need of some food and rest. Valentina bathed Lola first to remove the sand and dirt from her paws and fur. The pup hated baths but she knew it was going to happen regardless so she obediently sat there until Valentina was done scrubbing her. After a good rub down with the towel the dog shook herself several times and settled by the modern gas fireplace and took a nap.

Valentina bathed, perfumed herself and prepared to meet Marcus. Despite her business tone earlier with him she could not deny she was dying to see him, inhale his sexy cologne and kiss those lips. There was no disguising the intense feelings she felt for him. She wanted so badly to let him have her but she had to control these feelings until she was certain he truly had the best intentions for her. She dressed in a Lanvin, dove grey, cashmere sweater dress she purchased in Madrid along with taupe, suede, caged booties. She braided her hair when she went on her run because it was still moist and it was now dry with large sexy waves floating down her back. Adding a little makeup, jewelry and fragrance and she was ready.

Responding to a knock on her door, Valentina walked over to find Marcus holding a bunch of roses, trilliums and lilies in a tall vase. They stared at one another as she backed up into her room and he followed. He set the flowers down on the coffee table and then he took Valentina into his arms and kissed her mouth gently.

He stepped back and said, "Never do that again, not tell me where you are. I almost suffered a stroke from the worry."

He did not wait for her response but instead devoured her mouth and moved his hands up and down her back and hair. Valentina was overcome with the headiness of his kisses. She no longer cared and let Marcus take control.

Thanks to Lola, Valentina did not lose her mind completely. The little dog recognized Marcus and demanded to be picked up. He picked her up and kissed her cheek as well then carefully set her down. His eyes raked over Valentina's body and thirsted to taste and feel her naked in his arms.

Snapping out of her delirium and attempting to control herself Valentina quickly walked over to the bar and offered Marcus a drink but he came right to her and set the crystal decanter down. He took her face gently into his hands and said, "I need to get this off my chest right now. Diana Monroe came to see me after I angrily hung the phone up on her. She came to the office pleading for the master bedroom pieces and apartment. I refused and she started flirting with me. I walked past the open door the entire time she was in my office. Also, I had asked Melanie to walk in and out with bogus files a few times because I know how aggressive Diana can be. We walked out and she surprised me with a kiss. I pulled her off and we went downstairs together where I escorted her to the entrance of the store. You know Jamal the security officer? Well he saw me walk towards Union Square as she got into her car. That photo she sent you was a selfie and I had no idea she was even taking it! I spent all of 12 minutes in her apartment yesterday because my intentions were to kill her but I threatened her instead and don't ever intend to receive her again in my office. That is everything that happened, I am telling the truth."

It was honesty that Valentina saw in his eyes besides exhaustion and fear. Without uttering another word, they removed each other's clothing carefully at first, but as their passions flared their movements became more abrupt until they stood naked before each other breathing heavily. He grabbed her shoulders and pulled her towards him. Lifting her up by her bottom she wrapped her legs behind him and they stood there transfixed staring deeply into one another's eyes. Slowly he walked over to the bedroom and placed Valentina on the bed. He stood over her looking down at her beautiful breasts and sinewy body. She in turn brazenly looked him over to marvel at his strength and musculature. He started at her feet with kisses and his tongue. Valentina was lost in delirium as he traveled up her legs and settled on her mound. Here Marcus claimed his prize. He made sweet love to her folds and with his tongue and fingers made her come until her body jerked from the ache of an orgasm. She glistened with perspiration and grabbed his shoulders while he settled between her legs and entered her. Valentina cried out from his size and in unison they rocked until both were spent again and gasping for air.

Nestling her chin on the soft hairs of his chest Valentina caressed his cheek and whispered, "Marcus, let's go eat. I'm famished." He laughed and said, "But we just ate you beast. Give me a few okay."

Valentina sat up, "No silly, I mean food. I only had breakfast."

His fingers twirled around a long strand of hair that fell over her face. "Costanza fed me last night and I haven't touched water since. Let's go shower and eat."

Together they giggled as they soaped each other's bodies and thrilled with new sensations. With the water falling over them Valentina got on her knees and took his manhood into her mouth. She suckled him gently at first and then with a ferocity that had him moaning and jerking back and forth. With his hand on her hair he kept her in place as he came again. Helping her to her feet they kissed gently and he uttered softly, "I dreamt of moments like these so often with you. I want you always in my arms. My life without you is nothing and you can't imagine how happy I am."

Valentina kissed the inside of his hand and stepped out of the shower without saying a word. He stood there watching her dry off and wrap a towel around her body. At the door she turned and smiled to say, "I had no idea of what I was missing."

The concierge secured a reservation at the prestigious Lasart restaurant. The night was cool but they jumped right into a waiting car and headed to the two Michelin star eatery. Dining on classic Catalán cuisine of grilled Skate and sautéed seafood on a bed of tarragon leaves Marcus and Valentina shared this dish with gusto. To this they also added roasted pigeon for Marcus and a Dover sole for Valentina. They held hands and exchanged glances and smiles throughout the entire dinner. Marcus took her hand and kissed it gently, "I never thought I could feel this overjoyed. I love everything about you Valentina." She smiled and caressed his cheek, a gesture that he had quickly grown to love.

Valentina sipped more wine and said softly, "You crawled into my heart and made a little nest that grew into a place of hope and joy. I love you too Marcus."

There it was. She had said the words he longed to hear. He could barely contain his joy and wanted to embrace this woman and consummate their love again. The waiter came along with the dessert menu tantalizing them with incredible delicacies. They ordered one chocolate soufflé with ice cream. This was Valentina's opportunity to set some ground rules for their start on a new love.

"Marcus, what about work. We cannot let anyone know or we will both lose our jobs."

"Well, we can be very discreet for now but before we formalize our union I will hand in my resignation. Besides that monster Monroe already knows but I doubt she will talk."

"I wish you did not have to leave," she said sadly. They kissed softly on the lips and touched each other's faces and hair as new lovers do without shame in public. Marcus was never about expressing himself publicly but he wanted to shout it everywhere that she loved him. She shared further details to clear up any misunderstandings. "I also want to share a very rude message David left on my voicemail the other day." Marcus felt disturbed that her former boyfriend would leave her a message. "Let me hear it later so as not to poison this moment."

She appreciated how sensitive he was about wanting to keep their time together sacred and unspoiled. When the ice cream came they fed each other and kissed chocolate and ice cream off one another's lips. They looked around to see if anyone noticed and concluded they did not care.

Outside before getting in the car Marcus took Valentina in his arms and planted a seriously intense kiss. He looked down at her glazed over eyes and whispered, "I am going to enjoy making you cry out with joy again and again." Her blush was so pronounced that it made him laugh and kiss both her cheeks.

Dismissing the car they decided to walk instead. It was a good night for walking, as the sky was clear and the air crisp. They walked slowly along beautiful boulevards with chic boutiques and restaurants. Embracing one another their bodies felt perfectly molded together. Valentina inhaled his fragrance and reached up to kiss his cheek. The new grown hair on his face tickled her and she liked how his stubble was so becoming.

They walked along slowly and he kissed the top of her head numerous times squeezing her tighter against him and loving how they felt together. Finally he hailed a cab when Valentina complained of her feet hurting in her new shoes. In the car, he rested her feet on his lap and removed her shoes. He massaged her feet and took each toe into his mouth sending shivers up her leg that settled into a throbbing molten heat in her groin. By the time they reached the hotel their passion was so overheated that it took everything they had to keep appearances until they reached her room. Once inside he removed her clothes slowly and deliberately. He ran his hands slowly over her breast as he ran his tongue along her neck and tantalized her by gently squeezing her nipples. Picking her up effortlessly and carrying her over to the already rumpled bed, he bent over her and kissed her again in all her forbidden places.

She watched him slowly undress and admired his virility and musculature. He was strong and exactly what she liked, a muscled and lean body. Lying next to him he filled her body with more kisses, licks and tiny bites. They made love into the early morning hours until he was so spent that he fell out from exhaustion. Valentina quietly slid out of bed and went to the bathroom. She looked at herself in the mirror and smiled as her body was tingling from a mixture of exhaustion and sheer joy. Noticing her flushed cheeks and chest, Valentina looked and felt like she did when she was in her early twenties. Sex made her feel so womanly, young and desired. Everything about Marcus was a turn on for her. His hard body and generous lovemaking drove her mad. The way his hands moved over her with total command and how he filled her up completely to the point of delirium made her smile.

Whispering at her image she closed her eyes and prayed, *"Please God, let him be the one that will always love me and never break my heart."*

Valentina moved quietly across to check up on Lola and found her stretched out on the sofa looking directly at her. Valentina bent down and kissed the top of her head and ran her finger along her snout. The tail wagged wildly as she whispered to go back to sleep. Marcus slept soundly with one arm over his head. She climbed back into the bed and under the covers. His hand immediately found hers and he rolled over to kiss her again and again until their bodies melted as one and reached climaxes so intense that Valentina cried tears of joy.

It was raining softly in the early afternoon when they awoke and lay embraced in bed. Lola jumped up and snuggled along side Valentina, as she was accustomed to always do. They got up slowly and showered off the scent and stickiness of lovemaking from one another. It was more foreplay in the shower than actual cleaning but they were delirious with love and neither one wanted this to ever stop. Sitting in their cozy hotel robes, they ordered lunch and champagne to celebrate.

Marcus held her hands. "Are you happy?" he asked.

"Marcus, I am so happy right now. I'm almost afraid because, what if it changes when we return home?"

He studied the concern on her face and reached over to kiss her lips. Pulling away with their noses almost touching, he whispered, "No fuckin' way is anyone or anything interfering with our lives. I know this is real. This is so real it hurts. No more worries, okay?"

Valentina had never heard him use profanity but she smiled and said, "I just wish we could stay here forever."

He returned the smile and shook his head, "I have to head back tomorrow. Please come with me and this way we return together and I can sleep knowing you are safe."

Everything she wanted was right in front of her. She wanted to be wherever Marcus was because with him she was loved and safe. "Yes, I will return with you," she added softly while caressing his cheek.

"Oh, I forgot to have you hear that voicemail. I don't want these things lingering in our lives. This way you hear it and it gets erased. Nothing from the past to burden us."

She grabbed a piece of toast and got up to get her phone. The voicemail was played and Marcus erased it from her phone. He took her hand and sat her on his lap where he opened her robe and proceeded to make love to her. He placed her nipple into his mouth and suckled it while making love to her with his hand and fingers. She squirmed on his lap but he held her fast until he made her come in short gasps and in complete abandonment. He licked every finger on his hand and then took her mouth in his.

The remainder of the day was filled with the delights of exploring each other's bodies further like scrumptious meals. By the next morning, calls were made to cancel or alter plans. Marcus paid all the bills and escorted Valentina and Lola out to the waiting car that would take them to the airport.

Flying on a private jet was more pleasant and comfortable, especially for Lola. The little dog was allowed to walk around or jump on the seat of her choosing once the plane was airborne. This was a great relief to Valentina who hated how groggy she was after giving her a sedative. It was a pleasant flight with only one other passenger who slept the entire way. Valentina held Marcus' hand and slept on his shoulder. As she slumbered, he looked down at her ring finger and imagined how beautiful a cushion cut three-carat diamond would look on her slender hand. He wanted to lavish her with gifts and sent a thank you up to God for the gift of this incredible woman. This he knew was perfect.

PART THREE

CHAPTER 16

Girlfriends

The Meat Packing district hasn't been a place to pack meats in lower New York City for decades yet the name prevails. The former location of warehouses and tenements buildings now houses fancy boutiques, furniture stores and trendy hotels that attract a younger hipper crowd to New York. In recent years a famous above ground linear park walkway called the High Line was constructed that runs from 34th street to Gansevoort Street where the Meat Packing district had its start several centuries ago as an Indian Trading post. The masses walk this green space to enjoy an aerial view of lower New York City.

It was two p.m. when all four women converged onto Buddakan in the Meat Packing district. After exchanging hugs and kisses they ordered different cocktails and began their assault on Valentina. It was expected as she had just returned glowing and refreshed from Spain despite a bitter breakup a little over one month ago. Lauren being most outspoken charged ahead with her inquiry.

"So for a recent breakup you look rosy cheeked and I dare say there's a twinkle in your eye Valentina."

Valentina blushed brightly, "Stop, there's no rosy anything or twinkle. I just feel good. A little European air did wonders for me."

They ordered a second round of drinks and some Asian fusion selections from the menu. The conversations continued about Rocio's two children and Lindsey's latest foray with Botox but Lauren persisted on redirecting the discussion to focus on Valentina.

"Just for old times sake, did you know that your ex is in trouble at the hospital?"

Alarmed at Lauren's brazenness Rocio retorted, "Damn Lauren, you need to know when to quit."

"Oh hush, baby talk is so boring." Lauren rolled her eyes while Valentina remained focused on her champagne flute to avoid looking up, as she feared her excitement might shine through.

"Come on Valentina dish. What's new with you?" Lindsey added. "You go off to Spain for two weeks and you return radiant. What's up?"

"Maybe she had hot sex with a local man and is too shy to talk." Lauren laughed boisterously as did the others but Valentina smiled as she downed her second champagne cocktail.

"Shut up Lauren, all I am willing to share at this time is that sometimes we find love in places we never thought possible and sometimes it's right under our noses."

Rocio nearly spitting her cocktail chimed in giggling, "Oh, so now you're a philosopher."

Giggling the women waited on a response when Lindsey said, "Huh, she found someone yummy to help her get over dumbass David. Such a waste of a man!"

"Please, no mention of former boyfriends because I have started anew," insisted Valentina raising her hand to stop Lindsey before starting the third glass of champagne.

"Excellent point baby girl but just for shits and giggles he's been all over the news with that stuck up Diana Monroe and he looks pale and skinny, just sayin'," Rocio concluded.

"Oh well, that bleached blond would make any man sick with her demands and attitude. Vanity Fair did a spread on her in her house in Nantucket and there she was like some overfed cat lounging on her furniture. Enough about those clowns, now tell us about mystery man," Lindsey persisted.

"Well, he's an older man, and very kind; a true gentleman…" Valentina said but was interrupted.

Lauren nearly choked on her drink as she stated loudly, "Older? Like how old is old? Does the equipment work?"

Loudly they broke into a frenzy of giggles and cackles causing other patrons to glance over to see where all the noise was coming from.

Rolling her eyes Valentina whispered, "He's older by just ten years but he's young in body and spirit. Now enough with this intrusive investigation." She smiled shyly and drank the remainder of her third champagne cocktail.

"I love a good mystery and here's one for us to unravel," applauded Lauren enthusiastically with her jiggling gold bracelets making tinkling sounds that continued to bring attention to the four friends.

"No not happening! This is too new and he's not a rebound man so I don't want to jinx it any further with all this talk," declared Valentina.

After a little more playful prodding they gave up and spent the rest of the afternoon laughing and gossiping about fashion, babies, money and their love lives. Rocio was the first to leave the gathering as she had two small children at home with the nanny. Lindsey had a laser hair removal session but Lauren lingered.

Lauren was Valentina's friend since they attended The Villa Maria Academy together. Like Valentina, Lauren was tall with honey blond hair and brilliant green eyes that stood out against her dark caramel skin. She was addicted to her work as editor at Penguin books and had little interest in long-term relationships preferring casual non-committal dalliances.

Children bored her and she avoided them at all cost. Despite their differences and preferences, Valentina always confided in Lauren because she knew without a doubt that while Lauren was bold and loud she was also fiercely loyal and a true friend.

"Okay, so mystery man is from N.Y.C. because you said he was nearby."

Looking away wistfully Valentina added, "Funny thing is Lauren, he's right here and I have known him most of my adult life."

Lauren thought Valentina looked anxious and placed her French manicured hand over hers and squeezed gently. "Look at me girl. Take this leap of faith and forget everything about your past. That time is so over. Whomever he is I just want you to live the moment. Don't think about the future, those babies I know you are desperate to have or anything else. Just live this moment with mystery man and enjoy it because I have NEVER seen you so happily in love."

Lauren held up her drink to alert the waitress she needed another Bellini and waved her hand to suggest she was air signing her name for the check.

With wet eyes filled with tears Valentina reached over and hugged Lauren and said quietly, "I will live the moment, I promise."

They paid the check and embraced warmly. Lauren wasted no time in lighting up a cigarette and hailing a cab as Valentina walked for a while to clear her head from the flowing champagne and conversations of the afternoon.

CHAPTER 17

Poor Choices

The porcelain vase went crashing against the mirror missing his head by a few inches. David had ducked just in time to avoid being pelted by Diana. She was livid that his former girlfriend was the reason for her thwarted acquisition of the coveted art deco pieces. The bedroom alone was valued at over $100,000, the Kandinsky rug a cool $35,000 and the art pieces she had acquired from Sotheby's were left without the furniture that helped them stand out. Diana always got her way and David was the recipient of her fury.

"Diana! Have you lost your mind?" David yelled.

He made to leave when she came towards him and grabbed his shoulder, "That dumb ex of yours looks so innocent but she's the reason why I don't have this furniture or the apartment to launch my European collection. What are you going to do about this?"

She stood before him with her arms folded over her chest. David knew he had better say something she wanted to hear otherwise she might call the wedding off. He licked his lips and straightened his tie before he told her, "I'm going to have a talk with Valentina and convince her to sell this furniture to you. But sweetheart, promise me you will calm down, okay. Besides, it's just furniture, babe."

Diana realized David had no idea of the value attached to authentic period furniture, jewelry or anything with established provenance. She lifted her chin haughtily and glared at him to say, "Get this for me and we might have a wedding otherwise forget it. The showroom opening is in a few weeks and I want to own these pieces before they are displayed. Oh, and never call me babe. I'm not your stupid former girlfriend or some cheap chick."

She turned away and walked over to her bathroom where the interior decorator having heard the argument waited nervously to discuss the new marble floor in her Central Park West penthouse.

David had no idea of how devious Diana had already been with the photo and text. He was also unaware of how deeply frightened of Marcus Diana was and the lingering threat he had over her head. David felt pressure around his chest area as he traveled downward in the elevator. His mind raced as he planned how he would convince Valentina to change her mind. He determined to go see her immediately but Sebastian Turner the Hospital Manager was calling. David foolishly ignored the call. This was happening often now. Instead of doing his job he would hail a cab and run up to 138th and 8th Avenue. It was on the second floor of a darkened stairwell in the neglected walk up building that he knew where to locate the dealer he purchased his heroin and Oxycontin from.

David gave him forty dollars for four tiny wax pouches each with unusual names stamped in blue ink. He hid between the entry of a building and its stairs and sniffed all four bags while nervously wiping his nostrils with his fingers. This was the new world Dr. David Harrington had fallen into. He was often dazed, missed his appointments and the hospital was no longer interested in keeping him employed. The pressures of trying to be someone else and the demands of his career and fiancé had taken him to dangerous depths. Alcohol was no longer enough and he had decided that injecting the heroine would be his next step to feel a stronger high. It was a dark pit he was rapidly falling into and David was quickly losing all perspective. He was funneling thousands of dollars weekly into pills, liquor and whichever drug gave him the greatest buzz.

The drug problem started in medical school with uppers to stay awake all night for studying. Having access to medications and dispensable income from a generous trust fund made poor decisions easy to make. The casual drug use helped it escalate into what it had become. David was physically thinner and only cared to clean up when he had to make an appearance with Diana at some tedious fundraiser. When people remarked he volunteered a smart remark, "I have been a vegan for some time now," or "As a doctor I have to be in top shape to help my patients." David quickly ignored how dangerous a path he had embarked on and kept the few friends who knew of his problems at bay when they tried to help. To David everyone else had an issue and not he. Diana only cared that he always be impeccably polished. She may have wondered what was wrong with David but her selfishness was such that it kept her from caring Marrying him would have been easy for her because their families ran in similar social circles but she had no idea the danger he was in and didn't seem to care. To Diana people were dispensable and money could solve all problems.

It had been one month since Marcus and Valentina's return from Spain. Their days were spent preparing the new showroom and negotiating new acquisitions. In the office the atmosphere was exciting with the upcoming holidays and new merchandise that promised hefty profits. At work, Marcus and Valentina were the ultimate professionals. They exchanged information and did not let on that they were lovers. The nights were the contrary of the day with private dinners, intimate baths and extraordinary lovemaking in either home. Everything was falling into place for them to establish a life together with big and serious plans. These plans included children and a home to fit there new hopes and dreams. It was Thursday and the air was crispy and cold. All the store windows were decorated for the holidays. It was Valentina's favorite time of the year and her birthday was just a few weeks away. She had left her Tía Carmela a voicemail about having Thanksgiving at Marcus' apartment. It was Marcus' idea to include her closest living relative, making Valentina very happy.

On the mirrored foyer table in her apartment, she had placed a large crystal gourd filled with cinnamon scented pinecones when the concierge called up to her apartment. "Ms. Puig, Dr. David Harrington is here to see you."

Valentina wondered what he might want and was pleased she had her locks changed and had his name on an announce list in the downstairs registry. She responded quickly, "Uh okay, I will come down, thanks." Slipping into her Uggs and grabbing a sweater coat, Valentina went to the lobby to see what David wanted.

He looked distressed, thinner, lost and angry. She approached him confidently yet cautiously, "David, why are you here?" His mind was so preoccupied he had not noticed the elevator arrive. The doorman and concierge maintained their distance without taking their attention off the encounter. David spun on his heel and rapidly walked over to Valentina. The smell of liquor strongly offended her and made her recoil in disgust.

"You have to help me Vale, my fiancé wants some damn furniture that you are selling and she's really upset. Come on baby, for old times sake just help me out and give her the sale of this shit."

Valentina stepped back and wondered what she had ever seen in this pathetic man. He was weak and a coward.

She observed how he continuously scratched his face and squeezed his nose. The sight of him repulsed her as she took in what a creep he had become and to the obvious depths he had fallen into. No amount of money could give him class and in a way Valentina felt vindicated and relieved that she had been spared a future with David.

Speaking in a soft yet firm tone she said, "Explain to your fiancé that I do not buy or sell, rather the company does and what I do is acquire for the company and they sell it out. Even if I wanted to …" David interrupted her raising his voice, "No, you can make your boss sell them to Diana before they sell to the public. She collects this shit and it means a lot to her."

Valentina glanced embarrassingly at the doormen who watched cautiously from the corners of their eyes. She felt this sudden urge to race into the elevator. There was something about David's gravelly voice and demeanor that set her hair on edge. His eyes were wild and this frightened her enough to take several steps back as she said, "David, I cannot be of any help. This is out of my hands. You need to get help. You are on something that makes you crazy like this…"

He lunged forward and grabbed her shoulders and shook her hard shouting, "Listen you bitch you're just pissed that I left you for Diana."

Valentina screamed and broke away to flee when he grabbed her sweater and caused her to lose her balance and fall against two of the sharply edged marble steps leading to the elevators. Antonio and Jamie the doormen immediately apprehended David who fought them off. He loomed over Valentina now hurt on the floor holding her right side and closed his fist and swung hitting her in the jaw.

Antonio knocked him down and put him in a chokehold but David pulled out a switchblade and cut Antonio on the hand causing him to loosen his grip. David was moving towards Valentina now crying on the floor when Marcus opened the door to the building and with a swift twist to David's arm and kick to the back of the knee he collapsed to the ground. He shouted orders to call the police and an ambulance. Marcus looked over and saw Valentina crying in obvious distress but he refused to lose his grip on David and held tight as the enraged and crazed man shouted expletives and threats. David grunted from the pain to his knee when Marcus pulled him in an upright position and grabbed him by the throat to firmly state, "You come near Valentina again and I swear I'll hunt you down and kill you." Marcus was seething when David smirked at him and spit out, "Who the fuck are you?"

Marcus closed his fist and settled it on David's nose which cracked and started bleeding. David slumped to the floor crying out in pain and mumbled, "I'm sorry Vale. I'm so sorry." Marcus heard the police sirens and waited until they entered the building before he released his grip of David. Immediately he moved over and cradled Valentina in his arms.

Doctor David Harrington was arrested for assault, carrying a switchblade and possession of heroine and drug paraphernalia.

After three hours in the emergency room, doctors determined that Valentina had nothing broken with only several bruised ribs and jaw. It was about ten at night when she was released and returned home with Marcus. Upon entering her building Jamie and Antonio enthusiastically welcomed her and Marcus. Antonio had his hand bandaged but he insisted on pressing the elevator for them. They thanked both men and went upstairs. Marcus helped her start a warm shower and gave her two Tylenols with tea which helped take the edge off the pain in her throbbing jaw and sides.

The next morning Valentina awoke to the smell of coffee, French toast and the sound of distant chatter. Marcus was busy in the kitchen listening on low volume to ESPN on his phone. Remembering the events of the previous evening,

Valentina felt an anger surge deep within her towards David. It was hate towards him she felt yet there was an immense sorrow as well. All this thinking was threatening a headache. She went to inspect herself in the tall floor to ceiling mirror in the walk in closet. Just as she feared it revealed a large blue black, kidney shape bruise below her right breast. She recalled falling directly on the edge of the last marble step. The memory of his fist hitting her made her want to hurl. Valentina felt sick, her eyes were swollen and achy. Her jaw was an ugly shade of blue. There was no way she could shower, dress and go into the office. Reaching carefully for the phone she dialed Cece's number.

"Hi, boss, are you already at the office?"

"Actually, I won't be in. I need you to call Lindsey, Lauren and Rocio and reschedule the lunch we were having today at Nobu. Also, please cancel the reservation."

Cece was surprised and curious. "Sure, no problem, but can I do anything for you?"

Valentina was polite but needed to get off the phone because Cece could press or make her laugh which would only cause pain. "You know what, I'm good. It's just a woman thing; you know…I just feel really tired. I will see you tomorrow. Thank you Cece."

"Okay, but if you need anything just call. Feel better." Valentina pressed END and put the phone down. Cece heard the call drop and proceeded with her day.

Valentina brushed her teeth and went to the kitchen where Marcus had laid out breakfast for two. Despite herself she smiled at him and said in a groggy voice, "Good morning my hero."

Marcus gave her a careful hug and a kiss on the lips. He raged silently from within because he knew that for her sake he had to camouflage how he felt. After helping her settle into her seat he poured them coffee and served the French toast. Together they ate their breakfast. Valentina informed Marcus that she was not going to the office when he remarked, "Of course not. You will be sensitive for a few days so I want you to rest and relax."

Reaching for the phone she called Kevin the dog walker and made arrangements for him to come by to walk Lola. She knew he came to her building at 9:30 daily and it was now just a little past nine. He agreed to walk her dog and informed her that she would be one of three because the two pit bulls that belong to Doctor Walsh were with the family vacationing in Vermont. Hanging up Valentina asked Marcus, "Do you think he will remain in jail?"

"Without question unless some idiot puts up bail. But I can guarantee you that Diana will be the first person to disassociate herself from the good old doctor." He drank his coffee and added, "Are you worried he might return?"

Valentina moved gingerly and winced from the pain making Marcus look down into his coffee and pretend not to notice.

"I guess I am a little scared. I run in the park and he knows Lola. What if he follows me or worse has someone else try to harm me or my pup." She choked back a whimper and continued, "I hate him so much that I just wish he were dead."

Marcus came over and kneeled before her and tenderly held her face in his hands to say, "Listen, you cannot allow this to fill your heart with hate. I have already taken steps to correct your concerns."

"What do you mean?"

"Well, you should come and live with me."

Just then the doorbell rang. Knowing it was Kevin, Lola ran over to meet her friends. Kevin was a tall and lanky college student who also worked at the local veterinarian's office. He wore his sandy hair long and parted in the middle with a goatee that made him look like a throw back to the 70's hippie era. Valentina trusted and liked his gentle ways with dogs and especially with Lola. When the dogs saw one another they excitedly sniffed each other's bottom and played in the hallway while Kevin spoke to Valentina. Kevin took notice how Valentina, who was always polished and jovial, looked bedraggled and was distant. He asked, "I'll run her up to 86th street in the park if that's okay? And we will be back in about an hour." Valentina shook her head and quietly closed her door. One less thing she didn't have to do, walk Lola and bend her aching body to pick up the waste.

"Think about what I said," were the last words Marcus said as he kissed Valentina gently and threw his coat over his suit. He was late for a meeting he did not care much about because his first and only priority was hurting and frightened. After wiping down and feeding the spent dog, Valentina fell asleep on the sofa with more ice on her side. She had one dream and it was of her running away as David pursued her in Central Park. When she awoke she uttered to herself, "You'll never put a finger on me again, you creep."

Later that evening Marcus sat next to Valentina on the sofa. "Well, do I have to kidnap you or will you come live with me of your own accord?" Marcus popped a grape into his mouth as he watched Valentina drink some coffee, finish her toast and oatmeal.

Playfully feeding her grapes he smiled as he remembered how he dodged several calls from Diana Monroe and had instructed Melanie to never put her through again. Valentina wiped the corners of her mouth and feeling more like herself she said, "Well okay, but only for a short while until I feel better."

She watched him smirk and say, "No silly, I mean permanently." He flicked the tip of her nose with his index finger and leaned in for a kiss.

"I'm afraid not darling, I can only stay for a few days. I don't feel unsafe here in my home. He has been arrested and I plan to be in court to give my declaration." She looked him directly in the eyes and saw the frustration he cleverly suppressed.

Starting to get up he took her hand and she sat down again. Marcus needed to vent but she could not be the recipient of his frustration. Feeling he could not convince this strong willed woman, he resigned and said softly. "Fine my love, I will return in an hour. Is there anything you need from outside?"

"No, not really."

She watched as he cleared the dishes, flatware, cups and saucers and placed them carefully into the dishwasher. She appreciated how orderly and clean Marcus loved things to be because she was like that herself. Getting up, she walked over to him and wrapped her arms around his waist and kissed his neck and chin and said, "Hurry back. All I need from outside is you." They kissed passionately and Marcus left to pack his bags and return to stay for a while without her knowledge.

Valentina showered, changed into soft grey lounge pants and a silky, long sleeve, white hoodie. Wearing flip-flops she fixed up her bedroom and dabbed perfume on her neck and the inside of her wrists. She played some Bossa Nova and waited for Marcus to return.

Gathering several suits, accessories and varied clothing pieces, Marcus piled them all into his car and had Jimmy drive him over to Valentina's place.

The doorman Antonio and concierge Jamie were again on duty when they noticed Marcus' car pull up. Instantly, Antonio unloaded the bags carefully to not aggravate the bandaged cut on his hand while Marcus stopped to speak to his driver, "Jimmy, pick me up around 8:30 a.m. tomorrow." The loyal driver quickly responded, "Yes Mr. Napier. Will that be all, sir?" Marcus affirmed with a nod of his head. Walking over to the two building employees he spoke with more assertion, "Did the incident the other evening start here in the foyer or upstairs in the apartment?"

Valentina had not said how she fell, just that it happened as she tried to get away from David. The men explained how it all happened. Marcus gave each man his card and a $50.00 bill and asked them to contact him directly if David were ever to show his face around the building or street.

Antonio escorted Marcus with the bags up to the apartment and once inside, Valentina, surprised with all the commotion asked Marcus, "You're moving in I see. And what makes you think I am in agreement with this?"

He chuckled and admired how delicious she looked freshly showered and fragrant. Marcus walked over and gave her a hot kiss and squeezed her buttocks to his pelvis. "The only way I will sleep is knowing you are in my arms so you just have to deal with it," he said as he kissed her again and released her to walk away and retrieve his bags. He walked into her closet and pushed hangers over enough to hang shirts, pants and very expensive suits while Valentina just stood there with her arms crossed over her chest and with raised eyebrows while secretly loving his command. They spent the rest of the day having dinner, chatting and watching a movie on HBO.

Several days later David was out on bail. It was not Diana who paid his bond but a fellow physician who also enjoyed occasional hits of illegal substances. David faced several counts of assault, weapons possession and illegal substances. His life had unraveled and his once bright future was now in serious peril. The coveted position as an orthopedic surgeon was terminated. The once brilliant doctor was now a mess of a human being. David would not acknowledge his need to get help. Different social media outlets reported the arrest and subsequent firing which led to Diana Monroe cancelling all wedding plans. David was lost.

CHAPTER 18

Life Expired

Several weeks' later preparations for the gala showroom event for the numerous antique Art Deco pieces were underway at the store. Everyone was abuzz with excitement over the event and the approaching Christmas holidays. Elegant invitations were sent out to industry people in home furnishings, directors of the MET, MOMA and Frick museums were included and affluent New Yorkers who had the kind of money to spend on designer and period furniture. Michel Delón, a favorite designer of Marcus was hired to design the showrooms. Delón had an uncanny way of capturing the integrity of an era. From the sexy suede white wall coverings to the grey and white marble flooring, the showrooms looked extravagant. It occupied half of one floor in the massive store with each bedroom and sitting collection from Costanza's apartment displayed gracefully with artwork to complement the era. Models were hired to dress in modern cocktail garb and move about the settings striking poses while a DJ was instructed to play a combination of Dance Party and Lounge music juxtaposing the collections original 1920 – 1950's era. The anticipation for this evening was palpable and Valentina was the belle of the ball for securing the entire collection.

In her office, Valentina was on the phone speaking with Costanza about her trip to New York for the event while Cece was handing her messages. As she spoke to Costanza, Valentina saw that one of the messages was from David. She put the message on the side to address it when she was off the phone. It was seven p.m. and the day had been long and tiring when Valentina sat back in her office chair and stared at David's number.

She thought to herself, *I can't believe this fool? After insulting and knocking me to the ground and causing so much pain and distress, he calls?*

Her right hand went protectively under her breast where the kidney shaped black and blue was now a sickly yellow and beige color. Tearing up the small paper gave her some small satisfaction but curiosity was so powerful that she took the pieces out of the waste bin and checked the phone against the number she had for David on her mobile. The numbers were different and the one written on the paper had a Long Island area code. Using the office phone she dialed the number. As she waited for the call to connect she thought back how two weeks prior at the courthouse she declared along with Antonio and Jamie exactly what David had said and done. David was out after spending two days in jail and meeting the $50,000 bail. He had an expensive lawyer as did she but having to face him was unsettling. Marcus accompanied her to these proceedings and sat right by her side glaring at David. Despite all that had transpired it was reassuring to see how embarrassed and harried looking David was the entire time by keeping his head down and looking up only once to face Valentina and whisper, "I'm so sorry." She thought about the call he made and wondered why he wanted to speak with her?

After three rings she decided she was ending the call when he answered. His voice was gruff and hoarse as he bellowed out, "Hello!"

"David? You called earlier." His voice changed to one of anticipation and hope, "Oh I knew you would call baby."

Hearing him call her *baby* was an affront after how he had treated her. Valentina had an overwhelming need to yell and curse him but she restrained herself and asked, "Why did you call?"

David heard the coldness in her voice and put on his mellowest voice to charm her but his speech was slightly slurred and she heard it, "I'm a mess Vale and I need you. When we were together I was at the top of the world. I lost my position at the hospital but I need you and want you to give me another chance."

Valentina could not believe her ears. She concluded he was drunk or high or both and realized there was no reasoning with someone who was this way. Angry with herself for calling she sighed and responded, "Listen, you broke what we had to chase that woman and now you ask me to forgive you and take you back! No way, and one other thing, NEVER contact me again I have moved on and am very happy with my life now."

Fearing she might hang up he said loudly, "You know what, I never loved Diana. She's a selfish monster who called the hospital to report my arrest after I called her for help. That's what she did to me for not getting her what she wanted. I was wrong but where is your compassion? I lost my license and have lawsuits coming and going every which way. I remember you as having this big heart for everyone. It's my turn now for some Vale love."

Disgusted with his tone and slurred speech she simply said, "Goodbye," and hung up. The silence on the other end was the confirmation of this door also closing in on him. He became enraged and threw the phone against the wall and cried out expletives as he proceeded to destroy his apartment. Without Valentina he believed he was like a ship without a compass and he had to get her back. David had become an addict but he wasn't able to see this for himself. One way or another, he determined Valentina would be his again.

The evening was cooler but the streets sparkled with holiday lights as Valentina walked up Fifth Avenue with Marcus hand in hand. It was the Friday before Thanksgiving and she was tingling from the excitement. Marcus encircled her waist to press her body closer to his as they navigated up 51st street towards Sak's Fifth Avenue. Valentina was picking up her dress and shoes for the big event and dodging Marcus' questions as to their color and style. She wanted to look magnificent and the Marquesa red chiffon, one shoulder, draped gown along with Manolo Blahnik ankle strap pumps would help her achieve this goal. She had chosen a Kalgan lamb fur cape that was prohibitively expensive but Marcus had insisted on paying for her entire outfit as a present for obtaining the lucrative acquisition. After picking up the clothes they hailed a cab back to her place. Putting everything away Valentina picked up Lola and hugged her. She read the note Kevin, the dog walker left informing her of Lola's fun and successful park trip.

"You are such a good girl my baby. Come on we have to get ready to spend the weekend with Marcus."

Walking into her dressing room she picked out her weekender and packed it up with clothes she might need. At Marcus's house she already had a closet of her own with a dresser and vanity in the spacious spa like bathroom. Even Lola had a sizable section in one of the cupboards in the kitchen for her own food and treats. Life was so sunny for them that she worried something or someone might interfere and ruin their joy.

Settling down with a vodka gimlet, Marcus turned on the television to NY 1. After watching for a while he was about to turn it off when the news of a man jumping off the Brooklyn Bridge to his death came on and caught his attention. A photo of Doctor David Harrington was splashed on the screen followed by another of his engagement announcement with Diana Monroe. People were interviewed expressing shock and making banal comments.

Marcus turned off the television quickly and went out on the small terrace off the living room and thought about how to tell Valentina. Marcus knew this would make her very upset and this was something he didn't want to do but had to just the same. Valentina called out for him, "Marcus, I'm ready to go and I'm famished." He heard her call prompting him to lock the sliding doors, close the curtains and put his coat on.

Dinner by the fireplace in Marcus' kitchen was what Valentina loved and what he had yearned for so long. A tranquil life with a woman who appreciated simple pleasures was a dream come true for him. Shortly after, Valentina settled into bed to read a little while Marcus had a scotch out on his terrace. He turned to lean his back against the railing and to watch his future bride. This woman was everything and more. Besides her physical beauty it was her generous heart that he found compelling. He wanted nothing more than to spare her sorrow but life was a mixture of joys and pains and he had to tell her about David's death.

Walking back into their bedroom, he climbed into bed and embraced and kissed her neck. This led to their passions flaring and Marcus decided the news about David's death would have to wait.

The next day was brisk and walking Lola in Central Park was one of those simple pleasures of life that Marcus was grateful for with Valentina. She was always naturally pretty with little to no makeup in her neat workout clothing. He held her hand and they stopped by the carousel to let Lola chase squirrels around the area.

Facing Valentina and taking both her hands in his he said calmly, "Valentina, I heard something terrible on the news." She looked up to meet his serious expression.

"What news?" She looked for Lola and found her with her front paws standing tall against a tree staring up at a squirrel.

Taking a deep breath he said, "David Harrington is dead." Marcus knew it was blunt but there is no real way of saying something like this gently.

"What?" The look on her face was one of questioning.

"I heard on the news that he committed suicide." Her hands flew to her face as she started to cry. He held her in his arms and called Lola over. Lola came running happily over to them and when she noticed Valentina crying she cocked her head to one side and proceeded to jump up against her leg to be picked up. Valentina picked her up and hugged her saying to Marcus, "Oh my God Marcus, this is so terrible." They walked across to the house where Valentina showered and remained withdrawn the rest of the day wondering how she could have helped David.

CHAPTER 19

Big Ticket Soirée

Marcus was relieved when the weekend was over after two days of Valentina being withdrawn and contemplative. He called her aunt Carmela and informed her of the suicide. It was her comment about David being troubled and how relieved she was that Valentina was no longer a part of his life that Marcus appreciated the most. Driving in to work she was quiet but Marcus wanted to be certain she was okay.

"Will you be alright about what happened?" Marcus asked. Valentina was looking out the window and turned her head to look at him and said, "He was obviously in a lot of pain to do this to himself. I just feel bad that I could not help him." He took her gloved hand in his and said softly, "You know honey, a person in trouble has to be prepared to seek help. There is absolutely nothing you could have done to help him." She looked down and nodded her head in agreement with Marcus.

Taking notice that they were one block from the store they shared a kiss and embraced before starting their day. The car left Valentina on the corner of the store and went around the block to allow her time to get upstairs to her office. This way they did not arrive together and feed the rumor mills.

It was nine thirty a.m. and the 5th floor offices were abuzz with activity. Construction people were putting finishing touches on the showrooms, designers were bringing in merchandise to stage the different sets while the phones rang and people ran around with take out coffee cups in their hands. As Valentina walked through this melee those who knew her welcomed her warmly. She was all the rage as the woman who made these rare acquisitions possible. There was talk of a big promotion but it was all speculation. Members of the executive board of the company were very pleased that Valentina obtained such prestigious pieces and wrangled them away from other famous auction houses in New York, Spain and London.

For Valentina all this was a show and she enjoyed the attention and respect she was getting from those around her who understood the business of estate acquisitions. She walked past the showrooms that were sealed with large ugly tarp hanging from scaffolds. The furniture was covered and being protected from dust and curious eyes. She counted the sets and wondered why there were only four when there should be five. Each one represented one of four bedrooms and the large sitting room. Moving to the other side of the large showroom Valentina thought she would find another covered set but she did not. Now her curiosity was sparked and she had to be certain that every piece she secured was here. Walking over to her office she noticed Cece was chatting with another assistant and decided to wait a few minutes before calling her over.

Inside her office, Valentina dropped her bag onto the sofa and threw her coat carelessly there as well. She was still melancholy over David's suicide. Her thoughts took her back to when they first met in the emergency room of Lenox Hospital after she sprained her ankle running. She remembered how he showered her with affection at the start of their relationship and also how quickly his temper flared.

Many thoughts floated in her mind throughout the day until she finally came to terms with not feeling guilty. It was David who wronged her with another woman. Valentina consoled herself by knowing that in the two years she was David's girlfriend she was devoted and loyal.

The early evening hours brought more work as finishing touches were happening everywhere in the showroom space. Marcus sent Valentina a text.

Are you ready to leave? M

Almost, just getting my coat on and going for one last look at the showrooms. Meet you by Petco in about 10 minutes. V

Will do. M

It was nearing seven and the company was abuzz with people gathering packages and crowding the elevators to leave for the evening. Valentina quickly peaked into each set. Everything was in place, polished and looked amazing. Looking closer she could not understand where the most fabulously expensive pieces were from the master bedroom. She made a mental note to bring this up to Marcus, as she feared Diana had gotten her way and somehow obtained the pieces for her own benefit.

The streets were busy with tourists, shoppers and employees pouring out of the massive store and building. She went into the little alcove just inside Petco to wait for Marcus and took in the energy around her. People were everywhere as the Holiday tents were being erected in Union Square Park. His car pulled up and she stepped into the car and fell into his arms. After ten hours together in the same space and unable to express their love they unleashed it in the car. Jimmy drove along and peeked at his boss kissing Valentina. The loyal driver was pleased to see Marcus so happy. He liked Valentina, as she was polite and gracious and never haughty.

They sat in silence holding each other until Valentina asked Marcus, "Why aren't the master bedroom pieces on display yet?"

Marcus pulled her closer and said nonchalantly, "Oh I'm certain they will be in place by tomorrow evening. Don't concern yourself with anything, I've got this under control."

He followed this with a kiss to her lips that helped her forget all about period pieces and art. Marcus walked Valentina off to her apartment and quickly left with the excuse that he would return in one hour. It worked out for Valentina, as she wanted to walk Lola around the neighborhood and just be with her pup.

Marcus confirmed with Jimmy, "You know where the address is in the Bronx?" Confidently Jimmy responded, "Sure thing boss, my grandparents lived in Grand Concourse their whole lives. The Bronx is home to me too."

Jimmy drove all along the FDR drive and took the Willis Avenue Bridge to catch the 287 and finally the 95 New Haven North. He took exit 7 Country Club Road and made a right onto the road. He proceeded through the quiet neighborhood into the leafy street of Lohengrin where Tía Carmela lived. Marcus jumped out of the car and ran up the tall front steps and rang bell 2A in an elegant soft blue and white-shingled two family townhouse. A buzzer allowed him in and up the two flights of stairs where the pretty older woman waited for him. They warmly embraced as he took her bag and escorted her back to the car.

She excitedly asked, "Marcus I just love an adventure. She suspects nothing right?" He responded excitedly, "Not a thing. You and Costanza will stay with me. We will have Thanksgiving at my place and introduce Costanza to this holiday. Valentina has not a clue."

Carmela was tingling from the excitement and added, "I'm so glad you and Valentina are together. This will be a wonderful family weekend. God knows how I have prayed for my niece to have peace and a love like yours."

Marcus squeezed Carmela's hand and thought about how much he too had desired a life of peace and love with a woman like Valentina. He felt elated yet guarded because he would never be in peace until they were husband and wife and under the same roof.

At the townhouse, Marcus introduced the women to each other. They chatted about Valentina, and Spain then enjoyed seafood paella prepared by his housekeeper Sally. Costanza and Carmela got on very well and Marcus excused himself and went to spend the night with his beloved.

CHAPTER 20

Success

Diana Morgan spoke hurriedly into her cell phone with Nathan Woolsley as her driver navigated midtown traffic. Puffing nervously from her cigarette she sputtered to Woolsley the major stockholder of Infinity Acquisitions, "I insist Nathan, Valentina Puig must be transferred at once. She was rude to me and stole these period pieces out from under me. I was there first with Sotheby's."

Woolsley rolled his eyes as he held his arms out for his tailor to measure the width of his chest for a new suit. He sighed knowing too well the dramatics of Diana and responded to the anxious woman, "I'm putting you on speaker phone because I'm being fitted for a suit jacket. Now where were we, Ah yes, I believe you were being quite dramatic. Are you certain you're not just going through some bereavement issues over your recent beloveds passing and taking it out on Valentina Puig."

Her voice rose into a shrill that had both men look cautiously at one another, "Seriously Nathan, now you offend me. As if I cared anything for David Harrington. When he turned his life to vice it ceased to be my problem."

Losing patience with her callousness he remarked quickly, "Do not speak that way about someone who has died it makes you sound quite cold and…"

Interrupting him Diana said indifferently, "I am not cold! More importantly what are you going to do about that woman?"

Taking his time to light up a cigarette Woolsley responded after taking a long drag, "Absolutely not a thing. Valentina is an incredible asset to the company and she has done nothing wrong. See you at the party, bye now."

He motioned for his assistant to press END on the phone and proceeded with his day. Diana Monroe stared at her phone muttering, "Fucking fag wimp!" She threw her phone into her Birkin bag and sulked the remainder of the way.

Uptown, Valentina admired how beautifully the red Marquesa gowned flowed on her body. She was pleased with everything and at how elegant the soft chignon made her look. The diamond necklace and matching earrings that Marcus gave her finished the look and Valentina felt regal. Lola sat on the billowy duvet admiring her and barked when she heard Marcus put the keys into the door.

Marcus was rendered speechless as he looked upon Valentina's beauty. His emotions were raw and he had to keep himself strong because this would be a big night for the store, himself and Valentina. He found himself to be tongue tied until Valentina helped him out by saying, "You look perfectly dashing in your tux, my love."

Walking over to her he looked deeply into her eyes and saw his entire future shine back at him. The joy he felt was overwhelming and all he could do was take her hands and kiss them both and say, "We had better get going before I lose myself completely and take you right here." Valentina giggled and they walked out to the celebratory evening that awaited them.

Music played and crystal champagne flutes caught the light from dozens of chandeliers and glittered all around. The wealthy and glamorous were mingling and chatting excitedly. Everyone marveled at the pristine condition of the nearly one hundred year old furniture while others expressed an interest in desiring a piece or two. Beautiful flower settings fragranced the air as people laughed and exchanged air kisses.

When Diana arrived at the door with her invitation she was not allowed to enter at Mr. Woolsley's request. Exploding in threats and expletives she slapped the security guard who called the police and threatened her with pressing charges. Marcus and Mr. Woolsley were alerted about the ruckus at the front door and smiled to one another. Diana would have to wait until long after the party was over.

Valentina floated graciously about the crowd receiving accolades for her brilliant acquisition and work. Marcus called everyone's attention as the CEO of the company Nathan Woolsley addressed the crowd and introduced Valentina to all. She received an enthusiastic applause and kept her eyes on Marcus who clapped along with everyone else. Marcus addressed the guests and invited them to enjoy the evening with food, champagne and to feel free and dance.

Walking over to Valentina he escorted her to his office. She said nervously, "Marcus, this is not a good idea, people will wonder." Ignoring her concerns he opened the door and revealed his secret guests. When Valentina saw Costanza standing by her aunt she nearly fainted with joy. To her surprise both women were there and having a chat like old girlfriends. Kisses and embraces were exchanged as well as compliments.

Marcus embraced Valentina and said, "You were concerned that the master bedroom pieces you loved were nowhere to be found. Well actually, Costanza and I have been in some negotiations of our own. You see my love, that bedroom you wanted is actually yours now."

Valentina didn't smile right away. She processed what Marcus was saying and after a minute she looked at her aunt and Costanza's faces that were both teary eyed and then turned her attention to Marcus. When she saw the love in his eyes she embraced him. Now it was her turn to be tongue-tied. Costanza walked over and reached into her little velvet clutch where she pulled out the keys with the blue silk tassel. She placed them into Valentina's hand and closed it saying, "You have finally found love so now you two must live in love and build new memories."

Valentina stared at Costanza and the keys and then looked quizzically at Marcus who stood there smiling. He took her beautiful face and explained softly, "The apartment in Madrid is our European home now."

Valentina blanched and felt her knees wanting to buckle and managed to find a tiny voice to whisper, "Oh my God." That was all she said when Marcus kissed her gently as they were not alone and the two ladies applauded.

After a few minutes all three women embraced and dried tears of joy and followed Marcus to the party. The gala evening went smoothly with all but two pieces being sold. The Eames rocker was left behind, as was a set of sconces. Overall the purchase of the acquisition paled in comparison to what the store profited from selling these pieces.

Valentina carefully stepped into the car with Marcus and drove over to her apartment to continue celebrating their love, new furniture and home. She was overjoyed and could not believe how wonderful this amazing man of hers was. He thought of everything, from sending her aunt and Costanza invitations to the gala and putting them up in his home to surprising her with the prohibitively expensive apartment and the much coveted four-poster bed and vanity. It was starting to sink in that this chapter in her life, as she knew it was quickly ending and the future held endless possibilities.

Marcus removed her gown, hung it up and proceeded to finish undressing her. She did the same for him until they stood before each other naked and that was when all the pent up emotions of the evening flowed out of Valentina. He kissed away what joyful tears he could and made love to her until she fell asleep in his arms. Marcus looked before him and recognized how life had blessed him with all he ever wanted. He thought about what new adventures lay before him with Valentina and looked at the brilliant moon shining through the window and thanked God for this gift.

On Wednesday, Valentina stayed home recuperating from a champagne hangover while Marcus went to work. He had to be in bright and early to meet with the board and discuss his resignation. Two days before he called a meeting for Wednesday at eleven regarding his future with the company. Amidst boisterous protests of his leaving they reluctantly gave him a generous severance package and their best wishes. Nothing they said or did made him say why he had to leave but somehow they suspected it had to be because of a woman. Even Diana Monroe quietly sat at the other end of the long conference table and kept her feelings to herself. She nervously played with her pen following the embarrassment and hefty check she had to write to the security guard she slapped and cursed to keep her hide out of jail. Page 6, the celebrity news information page of the New York Post, as well as several other social outlets covering the Infinity Acquisitions bash, also photographed her explosive temper and poor treatment of the guard. All this bad press gave Diana a taste of her own medicine. The once coveted and respected heiress was now being seen as the witch she really was in life.

Thanksgiving was fun for Marcus because since his wife died eleven years earlier he had not celebrated the holiday. Valentina and Carmela took over preparing the turkey while Costanza made a ginger squash soup. There were other dishes and many of them with a Spanish flair that made Thanksgiving more delicious than ever before.

They sat down in the formal dining room that often went unused with a roaring fire as Lola feverishly chewed on a bully stick. Everyone ate and laughed. Marcus gave his staff the entire weekend to be with their families as he would not be around. Valentina did not know what he had in store but he did instruct her to pack a bag for a weekend away and bring food and comforts for Lola. After filling themselves with homemade apple pie the older women retired to the family room to watch television while Marcus and Valentina cleaned up the dishes.

By nine the next morning everyone was up at Marcus' request and ready to leave with their bags. Valentina tried in vain to get her aunt to tell her where they were going as they piled into a small SUV with suitcases and the dog. At Kennedy airport they boarded the private plane and left to Spain. Valentina continued to be the only person in the dark regarding the destination and for a while she showed a bit of consternation for being left out. After five hours, they arrived in Barajas and Marcus finally gave away part of his surprise, "Ladies, I hope to see you very soon." He winked at them as they hugged and kissed his cheeks. Valentina couldn't take it anymore and said with slight annoyance in her voice, "Okay, enough, where are we and why is everyone saying goodbye?"

Marcus laughed and it was her aunt who relaxed her with, "Querida, we are in Spain. While the two of you remain here in Madrid, Costanza and I will go to Barcelona."

Valentina relaxed and looked over at Marcus who raised both shoulders and just smirked. She walked over to him, shook her head and hugged him tightly.

They waited on the tarmac for the plane carrying the ladies to leave before jumping in their waiting car and to their new home in Europe.

El Portón, was exactly as Valentina had remembered but what she did not know was how beautifully painted in cool grays and decorated she would find her new home. Welcoming her in the foyer was the same elegant and enormous arrangement of white roses, trilliums and lilies that had become a trademark in their ever-blossoming love. Valentina excitedly moved from room to room with Lola at her heels barking with excitement and marveling at the beautiful furnishings in contemporary styles.

The last room to explore was the master bedroom. Embracing they kissed with longing and jumped on the new linens that dressed the magnificent art deco bed. Slowly Marcus removed her sweater, jeans and boots. Her underwear he peeled off with his teeth tantalizing Valentina with every pull and flick of his tongue. In the darkness of the room only lit with candles and the light that bounced off every tiny mirror inlaid in the wood, Marcus filled Valentina with his love and drove them both to that place of pure ecstasy that only lovers know.

The next day was sunny but cold. Christmas was in the air and Valentina awoke refreshed and thrilled to be alive. Dressing in her running gear she prepared Lola and went to walk and run her in the beautiful El Retiro Park. Taking in deep breaths to fill her lungs with air, Valentina recounted as they gently padded around the park and how life had changed for her in fewer than three months. Anyone else would have waited before making such serious commitments of owning a property together or starting a new relationship but for Marcus and Valentina these events in their lives could not be more perfect. Valentina did not think they were moving quickly because it felt so right. She thought about how they knew one another for just over a decade and the mutual admiration they shared. Valentina dared not wish for more because she felt that any more blessings would be impossible. She was grateful with having Marcus and being so loved. Looking down at Lola she smiled and thanked God, at her shiny new world.

The thick hot chocolate hit the back of her dry throat and made Valentina delight in its smooth texture and deliciously yummy aroma. Marcus was having coffee and together they enjoyed their new kitchen table situated off the double doors that led out to the little balcony. He looked lovingly at her to ask, "Are you happy?" Valentina looked at his brilliant eyes and smiled desperately trying not to tear up, as her joy was immense. He kissed her cheek, "Words are not needed. I have my answer in your eyes and smile, my beloved."

They explored Madrid and cooked meals for each other and planned how to use the massive balcony in the coming spring and summer. By Saturday, Marcus let her know about his resignation from the company. They went out late afternoon to walk the dog in the park and he figured this would be the perfect time. They walked as far as the statue of The Fallen Angel, Valentina's favorite in the park. Stopping to admire it he put his hands around her shoulders and whispered, "I resigned last Wednesday. I will remain until the end of December to groom someone for the position. Would you like to be that someone? The executive board mentioned you as their number one candidate."

Valentina looked at him in shock and immediately said, "Oh my God, I expected one of us would have to go soon but I'm sorry. About the position, it would be awesome but I prefer to remain where I am."

What she didn't want to say was that she wanted to start a family and taking on a demanding directorial position would be difficult. She wanted to express her desire to be a mother but did not want to scare him off.

On the plane back to New York they traveled without Tía Carmela. She called late Sunday evening to share how she was enjoying visiting with old friends and family and would stay for another week in Barcelona.

The week was uneventful but rewarding as Valentina received two floral arrangements from guests that attended the party, several invitations for lunch and dinner and a visit from one of New York City's most sought after bachelor, John Weiss, who was at the gala and could not keep his eyes off

Valentina. None of this went unnoticed by Marcus especially when the handsome John Weiss sauntered into the offices and every woman lost her head. It was more disconcerting when Valentina received him in her office but wisely left the door opened. They chatted but he got nowhere with his dinner invitation. Valentina made it clear she was not available for dinner or anything else. He gallantly removed himself from her presence and left the building winking to several ladies as he left.

During that weekend, Marcus playfully teased her about her new boyfriend but he knew very clearly that he had better make his intentions more solid and with a more obvious expression of love.

CHAPTER 21

Unexpected

It was December 10th and she was struggling with the back zipper of the sexy Diane Von Furstenberg star tiered sheath dress. Marcus would be there in no time and she still had to apply makeup and do something with her hair. After achieving success with the zipper but hurting her arm by twisting, she quickly applied a dewy tinted moisturizer. She brushed on mascara and a sexy mauve lip stain. A quick brush of her hair and she was as ready as she would ever be.

All day Valentina was feeling off. She wasn't hungry and she felt exhausted. Sleeping until eleven a.m., an unheard of event in her life, she called Kevin to come and walk Lola. Celebrating was the last thing she ever wanted to do because all she desired was to crawl into her bed as Marcus was opening the door and Lola noisily welcomed him.

Marcus noticed her quiet and tired demeanor. Walking over to her he embraced her tightly and planted a kiss on her freshly painted mouth.

"Oops," he said apologetically, "I did not mean to ruin your lipstick."

"It's nothing honey," she yawned as she retouched her makeup.

"Would you prefer we stay home, you sound and look so tired." Marcus asked with concern in his voice.

Valentina wanted to shout out YES, but after noticing the new and smart Zegna suit he wore just to celebrate her birthday she did not have the heart to disappoint him.

"I don't know what's wrong," she yawned a second time, "Perhaps I'm coming down with something."

Marcus helped her with her coat as she continued, "I'll be fine, just tired I guess." They walked out to the waiting car and twinkling lights of the night.

Marcus held her cold hand as they headed to Jimmy's Bar at the James Hotel on Thompson Street.

James Hotel is one of dozens of luxury boutiques hotels that have opened in the last ten years in major cities in North America and Europe. It boasts comfort, luxurious linens and elegant furnishings. Jimmy's bar is situated in the hotel and its clientele are the young and very fashionable crowd from Soho. With stunning views of the Brooklyn Bridge and Manhattan skyline it was always a crowd pleaser along with the absinthe-tainted cocktails.

The jovial crowd of friends and associates had taken over the best seats by the floor to ceiling windows. When Valentina and Marcus walked in they cheered and welcomed her with hugs and kisses. Cocktails and champagne poured freely throughout the night as everyone chatted and a few broke into bad renditions of songs.

By midnight, from Prohibition Bakery a colorful collection of tiered cupcakes were displayed before Valentina with a single silver candle at the very top. After a cheerful rendition of the traditional birthday song everyone waited while Valentina made a wish and blew out the tiny candle to the roaring cheers from the entire lounge. Cece was second after Marcus planted a sweet kiss on her mouth. The girl was giddy and her date completely wasted on one of the plum colored sofas.

"Happiest of birthdays to you," she said breathlessly with her generous bosom heaving up and down in the low cut wrap dress as she hugged Valentina. "Oh and you two make a very cute couple." Cece winked at Valentina and grabbed Marcus in for a tight hug surprising him and causing his eyebrows to nearly hit his hairline.

"Thank you so much," uttered Valentina and added, "Your date looks done for the night, let me call you a cab." Cece laughed uproariously and said quite loudly, "No way, we are going to stay at his place three blocks away but by the looks of him I'm not getting lucky tonight." She planted another kiss on Valentina's cheek and went off to dance with some other women by the bar. Gathering her clutch, Valentina thanked everyone she could and tugged at Marcus' sleeve to get his attention to say, "Marcus, let's go." Surprised at her desire to leave her own birthday party he asked curiously, "Are you sure? I thought we would be here a while longer? You alright?" She looked and felt exhausted and desperately needed to be in a horizontal position. "Yeah, let's go, I had a great time but I'm so tired." He escorted her to the coat check and down the elevator to the lobby. The cold air was refreshing and after hailing a cab she nestled into his arms and fell asleep.

Two days later a revolting wave of nausea hit Valentina like nothing she had ever experienced before. She felt sick and looked pale green. Reaching for her phone she dialed her doctor's number and made an appointment for later that day. Upon glancing in the mirror she was grateful Marcus was away on a business trip and would not see her in this sorry state. Her eyes did not shine and she looked spent. Feeling like she might have caught the flu she struggled to put her clothes on and noticed how tender her breast felt. She thought how awful it was to be sick during Christmas and how busy she was with gift buying and decorating.

Shoppers were everywhere and that crispiness to the air only felt in New York before Christmastime was evident. The cab took her to her doctor's office on 89th and York. The handsome lobby with modern furniture and travertine tiled floors shone with a huge Christmas tree decorated all in white and a large Menorah on the side sitting upon a table richly draped in white velvet. This was no time to notice décor but Valentina took notice just the same and then hurried to suite 207.

Doctor Julie Morgan's office was simply decorated in warm tones and tons of magazines in neat piles on a center coffee table. Valentina announced her arrival and took a seat. Feeling another wave of nausea she ran to the bathroom and hurled nothing other than bile. At this point the activity of hurling made her dizzy and clammy and she leaned against the wall to keep from falling down. With difficulty she exited and was grateful when her name was called before she had a chance to sit back down.

Into the ecru colored examination room with large anatomical posters entered doctor Morgan. She was petite, red head with bright green eyes and a warm smile. She took one look at Valentina and asked quietly, "Well, what has bitten you?" Valentina uttered, "Don't know but I think it's the flu." Doctor Morgan had her undress and put on a gown and proceeded to take her vitals. Blood was drawn and urine collected by the nurse. Doctor Morgan wasted no time in making her assessment after noticing how Valentina grimaced when she examined her breasts and abdomen. After dressing, Valentina and the doctor met in her office. Photographs of the doctor and two cherubic redheaded children smiled back along with diplomas and some knick-knacks from a recent trip.

"It's the flu right?" asked Valentina exhaustedly.

"Well I doubt this is a viral or bacterial infection. What you most probably are is pregnant," Doctor Morgan smiled warmly as she said these words.

In Valentina's mind the word "pregnant" bounced around. She was fuzzy and tired from feeling sick and could not process the full impact of her new condition.

The doctor noticed the glazed look on her patient and spoke softly, "Valentina, are you okay with being pregnant?" Noticing how Valentina was shallow breathing she called in the nurse to get water while she came over to hold her patients hand. The doctor gently continued, "Okay, you are pregnant and by my estimation around 8 weeks. I know excellent obstetricians that will see you through the next months or…"

Valentina looked up and focused her eyes on the doctor. "I'm pregnant and you're certain of this?" Doctor Morgan stood up to gather her notes and returned to sit next to Valentina. "All indicates you are. I did a urine test thinking you might have a UTI but it came back negative so I ran a pregnancy test and that was positive. So what's left is for blood work to confirm this but upon examining your breasts and abdomen they show signs of being pregnant. Again, I ask, are you prepared for this?" Valentina, despite feeling awful smiled and said, "So what I have is morning sickness although I'm feeling sick all day long?"

Doctor Morgan rose and returned to sit behind her desk. She explained, "Yes, but it could be a severe form of morning sickness called Hyperemesis Gravidarum or HG for short. What I want to do is call a doctor and get you into Lenox this afternoon just for a day or two. You're in danger of dehydrating and must get medical attention immediately."

Valentina was alarmed at the idea of going to a hospital but she understood how serious being dehydrated could be and reluctantly agreed, "Well, I need to get home and set up a plan for my dog and…" With the sudden awareness of the situation she burst into tears as her doctor gave her tissues and waited patiently. Without being pushy, Doctor Morgan excused herself to allow Valentina time to relax. Blowing her nose and taking a sip of water Valentina composed herself enough to take her bag and leave.

She met the doctor at the front desk who discreetly informed her, "Doctor Michael Olivares is an excellent obstetrician at Lenox. He expects you at his office in the hospital by four p.m. and it is now one p.m. Can we call someone for you or can you manage on your own?"

Valentina added quickly, "I came this far on my own, I will be there at 4 p.m. Just do me a favor and forward blood tests to the doctor so I'm not pinched again, please." The doctor smiled and nodded her head affirmatively then she asked the receptionist to call Valentina a cab.

Her world was spinning before her as she left her apartment with an overnighter and instructions for the concierge regarding Lola. Calling Marcus was the right thing to do but it would only make him panic and rush back from his business trip. She was feeling like too much information was coming her way and all she wanted to do was sleep and cry. Being pregnant was what she always wanted but a hospital and being alone were never included with this plan. Taking stock of her situation she called Cece from the cab to let her know she would be out the rest of the week with the flu. No sense in getting people talking and worried, she thought to herself.

At Lenox Hospital, Valentina went to the office of Doctor Olivares. She walked into an office where three other very pregnant women were already waiting and took a seat as far away from them as possible. It was here when she realized just what was happening and another wave of tears took over. Her mind was racing with thoughts about her future.

Oh my God, What I always wanted might be and I'm not even engaged. Marcus has to know but when because I don't want him to feel pressured to marry me.

Looking down at her flat stomach she instinctively placed both hands over it as if to protect the precious cargo within.

While controlling the constant desire to hurl and the threatening tears as best she could she went over when the receptionist called and escorted her to room B where the nurse had her remove all her clothing and put on a gown.

Feeling cold and scared she waited until a short man of around 60 with a fully trimmed, silvery, grey, beard walked in. He had a genuine smile that helped Valentina relax a little. After placing reading glasses on he read the report that had been emailed from Doctor Morgan's office. The doctor looked up at Valentina over his glasses and announced, "I need to do a pelvic exam to confirm your pregnancy." Without expecting a response from Valentina he and his nurse proceeded to position her on the table when another bout of nausea hit Valentina only this time she nearly fell off the table with the force of the stomach contractions. Nurse Olga helped her spit up into a pan and took a moistened towel to pat down Valentina's reddened and clammy face.

The doctor efficiently and quickly concluded his exam and declared she was indeed pregnant. In seconds the nurse set up an IV drip in Valentina's vein and unceremoniously stuffed her belongings into a white plastic drawstring bag with blue letters denoting the name of the hospital and below it Maternity Wing.

Before the hour was done, Valentina was alone in a semi private room with a view of Lexington Avenue. With her phone securely by her left hip she placed her hand over her abdomen and dozed off thinking of her and Marcus' baby to a much-needed nap. It was evening when she was awakened by a tray of food being placed on her bed table. The unmistakable smell of hospital food made her stomach roll. She pushed the table away against the wall and closed her eyes again.

The cell phone anxiously vibrated against her thigh. Ignoring the abhorrent scent coming from the food on the tray, Valentina answered Marcus' call. She had resigned herself to having to share some of the news because not telling him would make him angry and they had promised never to keep anything from one another.

Answering the call Valentina didn't have a chance to say hello as Marcus cheerfully asked, "Hey gorgeous, what are you up to?" Valentina told Marcus everything except being pregnant.

"Remember how I have been feeling awful lately, well, I'm at Lenox for some IV fluids to prevent dehydration. Doctor Morgan is being overly cautious and I should be out soon."

Marcus was silent on the other end, "Marcus, you there?" she asked.

He snapped out of his concern and added, "I'm sorry I'm not there with you. I can leave tonight and be…"

Interrupting and speaking firmly, "Marcus, you don't need to rush back, I almost didn't tell you because I knew you would go nuts. I'm okay, come back Friday and we will meet at my place alright?"

Marcus had to conclude this business trip on a high note as he was seeking a directorship with Christie's.

"Are you sure of this Valentina? I don't like that you are alone. Call Tía Carmela or one of your girlfriends."

Valentina wrinkled her nose at the tea she took a sip from before responding, "Silly, I prefer having this quiet time. I'm leaving now to go eat and I better not see you until Friday so no dropping your work to come and play nursemaid."

"You are headstrong Valentina. I will call you when tomorrow's meeting concludes around 1 p.m. I love you so much," Marcus said lovingly.

"And I can't wait to be in your arms and whisper those same words in your ear," she whispered into the phone as she was feeling sick again.

Valentina knew Marcus would feel better hearing her sound sexy and secure instead of frightened and needy. Marcus blew a kiss into the phone and Valentina returned one and then ended the conversation.

For the next two days, Valentina was pumped with fluids and given medication to ease the nausea. She received a visit from Doctor Olivares on Thursday morning. He smiled warmly and said she could go home which was music to her ears, as she desired a bath and to be with her dog. There was much to do now that she was pregnant. The short time in the hospital helped Valentina prioritize her immediate future. She was planning just how to break the news to Marcus.

Doctor Olivares had a final warning for Valentina, "You are considered a high-risk pregnancy because you are 36 years old and experiencing HG. You will need to be in contact with my office more often. I want to see you there next Tuesday morning. Oh and I'm afraid that for the next days until I see you again you cannot return to work."

She took it all in and nodded. What else could she do when her little baby was at risk? Her heart was overflowing with love. A nurse helped her into her clothes and she signed a waiver to leave the hospital alone. As she was wheel chaired to the front door to the waiting cab she thought of how crazy everything was now for her. Her life would never be the same from this moment on and while it frightened her terribly Valentina felt that her heart could not hold more joy. Sometimes the best-laid plans take detours in light of new developments and a baby was certainly a major situation in any life. For Valentina, it was the ultimate goal in her already privileged life. She had it all and a baby would make it complete and sweeter than anything else ever could.

Standing nude before her full-length mirror she looked to see if her abdomen showed signs of a baby being formed. Her strong and flat stomach showed no sign but she certainly felt differently. Besides the dark circles under her eyes from days spent vomiting and being several pounds lighter due to little or no food all she noticed were her breasts looking slightly larger and the nipples extended and red. The slightest brush against her own clothing provoked discomfort but she was certain Marcus would think it just grand that her breasts were larger. Throwing on a pair of jeans and a black cashmere turtleneck, Valentina waited for Marcus to arrive.

She decided that telling him about the baby was the right thing to do and felt confident this would not be a problem for him. He had been clear that he wanted a family but they weren't married nor had he proposed. This reality bothered Valentina because she did not want his marriage commitment because of the baby; she had to know that in spite of this new development he wanted to marry her.

Hunger was no longer an issue for Valentina because food repulsed her and threw her into nauseous episodes that left her weak and anguished. Tomato soup seemed to work, as did vegetable broth along with Ak-Mak crackers. No other food could be entertained including her beloved chocolates or champagne.

Lola went racing and barking to the door as Marcus squatted down to embrace the happy pup. He walked into the kitchen where Valentina was stirring a pot of organic tomato soup from Trader Joe's. She looked up and smiled but he said nothing as he saw how gaunt she looked and took the wooden spoon off her hand and set it down. Taking her by the shoulders he embraced her gently at first and then firmly while uttering softly, "I missed you so much…" She cried out and he released to see her grimace.

"What hurts? Please tell me," Marcus asked anxiously.

Looking back at her tomato soup to disguise the tears that hovered on the edge of her lashes she whispered, "My entire body is on pins and needles but I'm feeling better."

Marcus took off his hunter's coat and threw it carelessly on a stool. He stood next to her and said, "Okay, so let's go out and get you some real food."

The thought revolted Valentina as she said; "Actually, all I can keep down is this with crackers." He looked around to see the crackers and a small bowl with a spoon at the place setting.

"Is there enough for me?" He was hungry but would not tell her as she was behaving finicky about everything.

"Of course there is, just grab a bowl and I will serve you too. But you look hungry so you should make a grilled cheese to go with that," she said sweetly as she wondered how she would survive the need to hurl with the smell of melting cheese.

Marcus said casually, "I had a nice lunch before getting on the plane but the crackers and soup will do. Is there anything you would like to do after we eat?" he asked.

"I was hoping to walk Lola around the neighborhood. I know it's cold but I haven't walked her in a couple of days and I need this as much as she does."

Valentina took the ladle and poured soup into each bowl. She also served Marcus a glass of Pinot Grigio and warm Jasmin tea for herself. They proceeded to eat while stealing glances at each other. She wanted to blurt it out but didn't want to spoil the surprise by telling him in the kitchen. She thought about this again and concluded to wait to tell him in a more proper manner.

The air was cold and the sky clear and black as they walked embracing each other slowly up 72nd on 3rd ^{Avenue}. On 73rd street they made a right turn and walked down to 1st Avenue enjoying how Lola wiggled her bottom when she walked. They stopped in front of the Buckley elementary school. Marcus took her face in his hands and kissed her softly on the lips. When he looked at her face her eyes remained closed and she circled her arms around his waist and whispered in his ear, "I love you so much. How do you feel about being a daddy?"

Marcus stared into her face that now had tears flowing freely down her smiling cheeks. He stood there with his mouth open and kissed her again choking on his emotion and joy.

"I think my heart will burst Valentina. This is the best news I could have heard." He embraced her tightly but she grimaced and pulled away.

"What?" he asked with concern.

She pressed her arms up to her chest to relieve the pain and laughed as she told him about her strange condition.

"Well, I have a weird case of extreme morning sickness called HG, I can't remember the name the doctor said but I was in the hospital due to this." Marcus stood frozen and attentively listened as she continued, "I may need to go back in if I start vomiting uncontrollably and my breasts hurt like Hell. So you can't squeeze me for now." She said these last words as she laughed and chirped, "Oh and I am exactly 9 weeks pregnant today and our baby is due sometime in late June." She took a deep breath and looked at the school longingly. Marcus followed her eyes and embraced his beloved and then led her to the warmth of her apartment.

After a gentle romp between the sheets he walked over to his coat and took out a box. Wearing their robes with hair tousled and smelling of love and sex he proposed to Valentina and set a three-carat cushion cut canary diamond on her finger. He lifted her chin and said, "I wanted to propose on Christmas day but from now on everyday will be like Christmas for us." Her immediate tears of joy were all the confirmation Marcus needed as he kissed her again and again and again.

CHAPTER 22

The Greatest Acquisition

They danced into the early morning hours celebrating their wedding at the newly reopened Rainbow Room. Valentina looked illuminated from within wearing an empire waist Marquesa bridal gown from the spring collection. Marcus danced with his bride and their joy was evident to all as they both wore permanent smiles on their faces. It was now March and she was just starting to show but the beautiful gown flowed and disguised her condition. Friends and the few family between them came out to celebrate as they took their vows in the restaurant with the lights of the iconic New York City skyline twinkling around them.

They were living together at Marcus' lavish townhouse while Valentina's apartment was sublet to two recent female graduates from Marymount Manhattan College. Their lives could not be more perfect and they knew it. Not taking anything for granted they thanked God daily for all their blessings.

With Marcus' new position at Christies he was a liaison between the New York auction house and several European markets, Madrid being one of them. He set the deal up himself to be able to live part of the year with Valentina in the capital of Spain.

Four months later on a bright sunny day in Madrid, Valentina was very pregnant as she walked back to the apartment with Lola from a walk in El Retiro Park. Their much-anticipated baby was due in two weeks and she and Marcus were putting the finishing touches on the nursery.

Marcus stood at the doorway watching as two student artists commissioned from the Marbella Design Academy painted the pastoral scene in the nursery. His eyes scanned the muted earth tones of hills and flowers with farm animals peacefully grazing. The pretty fresco gave Marcus a sense of peace and calm. The artists looked up when Marcus stopped talking into his cell phone. The young man with a goatee and man bun popping from the top of his head asked with a smile, "Señor, está todo bién?" Marcus shook his head to imply all was well and smiled. Returning to the call on his mobile he concluded a negotiation of the acquisition of two priceless Erté vases with a collector in Belgium. Hearing the front door open prompted him to end the conversation as Valentina entered the foyer. He met her there and kissed one another on the lips.

"Did you have a good walk?" he asked as she removed her sneakers and padded over to clean up Lola.

"It was great and not a soul around just the way I like the park, very quiet and all for Lola and me. Is the nursery mural ready?" Valentina asked excitedly. Marcus leaned against the doorframe to watch her carefully clean Lola's pads with wipes.

"Yes, the painting is just about done." Marcus felt a stirring of happiness in his heart. He gazed upon Valentina in wonder.

She looked up to catch him staring at her, "And what are you looking at?"

Feeling blessed and filled with emotion he responded softly, "Of all the acquisitions I have obtained in my life nothing compares with you. You are my greatest acquisition. I'm the luckiest man in the world."

Valentina walked over to him and wrapped her arms around his neck and gave him a kiss with all the love she had in her heart. Leaning her head back she smiled up at him and said, "No, we are the luckiest man and woman in the world and don't you ever forget it mister. Now let's go check out the nursery for our baby girl."

End